OBLOMOV

By

IVAN GONCHAROV

Adapted for the stage

By

STEPHEN WYATT

ISBN 978-0-9556868-6-3

CHARACTERS

OBLOMOV
ZAHAR
TARANTYEV
DOCTOR
STOLZ
OLGA
OLGA'S AUNT
AGAFYA
NICOLAI
BAILIFF
NANNY

Doubles –
AUNT / AGAFYA / NANNY
DOCTOR / BAILIFF / NICOLAI

SETTING

A LARGE UNTIDY BED AND WHATEVER ELSE
SEEMS NECESSARY

THE PLAY IS SET IN AND AROUND ST.
PETERSBURG IN THE 1850s.

An earlier version of this adaptation was broadcast
on BBC Radio 4
With Toby Jones as Oblomov

ACT ONE

(OBLOMOV WRAPPED IN HIS
SHABBY DRESSING GOWN LIES
ASLEEP IN HIS LARGE UNTIDY BED
SURROUNDED BY DARKNESS. HE
TOSSES AND TURNS FITFULLY.
A FIGURE APPEARS OUT OF THE
DARKNESS BEHIND HIM. A ROUGH
MIDDLE-AGED PEASANT - HIS
BAILIFF.
THE FIGURE SPEAKS:)

BAILIFF: "Dear master, I regret to inform you that
             everything is not well on your estate. The
             old people don't remember there having
             been such a drought. The spring crops have
             burned up like fire. Sadly this year we will
             be sending you some two thousand roubles
             less than last year, our father and
             benefactor…"

             (OBLOMOV MUMBLES IN HIS SLEEP.
             THE FIGURE VANISHES.
             OBLOMOV OPENS HIS EYES,
             YAWNING.)

OBLOMOV: Mmm, I should get up. Things to do. Letters
             to write. Decisions to make. Time and tide
             wait for …

             (HE GIVES A COLOSSAL YAWN AND
             CLOSES HIS EYES AGAIN. IDYLLIC
             COUNTRY MUSIC CREEPS SOFTLY IN.
             OBLOMOV SIGHS CONTENTEDLY.)

OBLOMOV: Ah, yes, how I still love you, my home, my
             lovely childhood home, my Oblomovka.

             (ANOTHER FIGURE LOOMS OUT OF
             THE DARKNESS – HIS CHILDHOOD
             NANNY.)

1

OBLOMOV:	How I wish everything there was the way it was when I was a little boy…
NANNY:	(SOFTLY CALLING HIM) Ilya! Ilya!
OBLOMOV:	Oh, good - here comes nursey! She wants to put my stockings on but I won't let her! I kick my legs and say I don't want to get up. I'm never going to get up. And nursey says I'm a naughty boy but she's laughing and ….

(SUDDENLY THE MUSIC CUTS OFF. THE FIGURE VANISHES. LIGHTS SNAP ON. OBLOMOV'S OLD AND MALODOROUS SERVANT, ZAHAR, IS SHAKING HIS ARM.)

ZAHAR:	Ivan Ilyitch! Ivan Ilyitch!
OBLOMOV:	(SUDDENLY AWAKE) What is it? Where am I?
ZAHAR:	In your flat in St. Petersburg. Where else? You called me.
OBLOMOV:	Did I? What for?
ZAHAR:	How do I know? I'm not a mind reader. (LEAVING) Call me again when you've remembered. I've icons to polish.
OBLOMOV:	No, wait, Zahar!
ZAHAR:	(WEARY SIGH) What is it?
OBLOMOV:	I've just remembered!
ZAHAR:	Remembered what?
OBLOMOV:	(STILL YAWNING) What I wanted you to do. I can't find that letter I received yesterday.
ZAHAR:	Which letter?
OBLOMOV:	The one from my bailiff at Oblomovka.
ZAHAR:	What was it about?
OBLOMOV:	How do I know? I'd only read the first few sentences and they were so depressing that I put it down.
ZAHAR:	Well, I've not seen it.
OBLOMOV:	It must be somewhere. Look in the waste paper basket.

(ZAHAR RELUCTANTLY SEARCHES.)

OBLOMOV: Or perhaps it's behind the sofa.

(GRUMBLING, ZAHAR CONTINUES
HIS SEARCH)

OBLOMOV: The back's still not been mended. Why
               haven't you sent for the carpenter? You
               broke it.
ZAHAR: (STILL SEARCHING) I did not. It broke by
               itself. Anyway, the whole thing's falling
               apart.
OBLOMOV: Well, never mind, is the letter there?

(SLOWLY ZAHAR EMERGES WITH
SOME TATTERED OLD PAPERS.)

ZAHAR: Here.
OBLOMOV: No, those are old ones. (WEARY SIGH) I
               suppose I shall have to look myself when I
               get up.
ZAHAR: (MUTTERING IN RETREAT) If you get
               up.
OBLOMOV: What did you say?
ZAHAR: Nothing. (LEAVING) I just wish I was dead
               and done for.

(PAUSE. OBLOMOV STARTS TO
SNEEZE)

OBLOMOV: Zahar!
ZAHAR: (RETURNING) What is it now?
OBLOMOV: (HOLDING BACK SNEEZE) Where's my
               handkerchief?
ZAHAR: How do I know where your handkerchief is?
OBLOMOV: I haven't seen it for two days. Do be quick!

(ZAHAR RELUCTANTLY SEARCHES
THE BED AS OBLOMOV TRIES TO
HOLD BACK HIS SNEEZE)

ZAHAR: Ah, there it is.
OBLOMOV: (SNEEZING) Too late!

ZAHAR:	You're lying on it.
OBLOMOV:	Surely not, I –
ZAHAR:	You can see the end sticking out.

(EMBARRASSED PAUSE. OBLOMOV
FEELS AROUND AND FINALLY
LOCATES THE HANDKERCHIEF)

OBLOMOV:	Can't imagine how it got there. (WIPING HIS NOSE) But then, of course, I wouldn't need it if the flat wasn't so full of dust. Just look at the samovar – it's a disgrace.
ZAHAR:	It's all very well for you to criticise but when do I get a chance to clean the place? You're always at home and lying in bed.
OBLOMOV:	Sometimes I go to the theatre or – or go and see friends. You could clean the flat then.
ZAHAR:	Oh, very helpful! How can I clean it at night?
OBLOMOV:	Don't you realise that dust is a breeding-ground for moths?
ZAHAR:	And what about the fleas? I've got them all over me.
OBLOMOV:	That's nothing to be proud of.
ZAHAR:	Well, it's not my fault there are bugs in the world. I didn't invent them. Or mice. We've got them as well.
OBLOMOV:	So how come other people don't have these problems?
ZAHAR:	Search me.
OBLOMOV:	Because they have servants who sweep their flats!
ZAHAR:	Even if I did clean the flat today, there'd still be more dirt tomorrow.
OBLOMOV:	Well then, you'd have to clean it all again.
ZAHAR:	Clean the flat every bloody day? I'd sooner be dead.

(ZAHAR LEAVES. OBLOMOV YAWNS)

OBLOMOV:	I should be getting up, I really should. And I must find that letter. (YAWNS) The trouble is – I have so many good ideas that my brain

gets swamped. Then I think I must write
them down and I think –

(ANOTHER YAWN. THE OPENING
MUSIC CREEPS BACK IN)
(THE LIGHTS DIM. THE NANNY
APPEARS AGAIN.)

OBLOMOV: I just wish I was back in dear old
             Oblomovka as it was when I was a boy!
             Amidst those bright landscapes. And happy
             uncomplaining peasants.
NANNY: (FROM THE DARKNESS) Ilya! Ilya!
             Come along!
OBLOMOV: (RAPT) And now nursey's going to take me
             to see my mother. And she's kissing me and
             stroking my hair and asking if I'd slept well.
             Well, of course, I had and –

(A CLOCK STARTS TO STRIKE. THE
LIGHTS SNAP ON. OBLOMOV IS
SUDDENLY AWAKE)

OBLOMOV: Oh, my goodness, eleven o'clock!
             (CALLING) Zahar! Zahar!
ZAHAR: (RETURNING) What now?
OBLOMOV: Is the hot water ready?
ZAHAR: It's been ready for ages.
OBLOMOV: Why didn't you tell me before? I'd have
             been up hours ago
ZAHAR: Maybe you ought to take a look at these.

(HE PRODUCES A LARGE FISTFUL OF
BILLS)

ZAHAR: The butcher, the greengrocer, the baker, the
             laundress – you name it.
OBLOMOV: Why didn't you give me these separately
             instead of producing the lot at once?
ZAHAR: Because you always say to-morrow will do.
OBLOMOV: Well, won't it do now?

ZAHAR:	<u>(EXASPERATED)</u> No, they won't give any more credit. This is the first of the month – remember?
OBLOMOV:	Oh dear. Put the bills on the table and I'll have a look at them later. The water's ready, you said?
ZAHAR:	Yes.
OBLOMOV:	Then it's time to get up!

<u>(A LONG EXPECTANT PAUSE)</u>

ZAHAR:	There's something else I should mention.
OBLOMOV:	I am trying to get up.
ZAHAR:	This morning, while you were still asleep, the landlord's agent sent the porter to say they want the flat back.
OBLOMOV:	Well, what of it?
ZAHAR:	It means we'll have to move,
OBLOMOV:	Just tell them we're going to move. In our own good time.
ZAHAR:	They said they're sick of your promises. If you don't go soon, they're going to the police.
OBLOMOV:	Let them!
ZAHAR:	But –
OBLOMOV:	Don't interrupt, I'm attempting to get up. Just tell them we'll move in a few weeks – when the weather gets warmer.
ZAHAR:	The agent says the workmen are coming in a fortnight's time to start the rebuilding work. They want you to move to-morrow or the day after.
OBLOMOV:	To-morrow! Perhaps they'd like us to move this very minute.
ZAHAR:	I'm sure they'd love it.
OBLOMOV:	Just point out to them that we've lived here for years and I've always paid the rent.
ZAHAR:	I've tried that.
OBLOMOV:	And what did they say?
ZAHAR:	They want to knock this flat and the doctor's next door into one before the landlord's son gets married. You could at

	least write to the landlord. Then he might start on the doctor's flat first.
OBLOMOV:	(RELUCTANTLY) Oh very well. I'll write to him once I've had my bath and – written up my notes. And found the bailiff's letter. (EXASPERATED) Really, I have to look after every little trifle myself!

(A DISTANT DOOR BELL GOES)

OBLOMOV:	Oh my goodness, a visitor already and I'm not even out of bed.
ZAHAR:	(LEAVING) I'll go and see who it is.
OBLOMOV:	And I must – oh dear me -

(A BIG YAWN. HE SLUMPS BACK IN BED)

OBLOMOV:	Why must I do anything? What is the point? People dropping in to see me, what exactly are they achieving by their activity?

(HE YAWNS AGAIN)

OBLOMOV:	Just thinking about what they do for no good reason is enough to make you feel tired. I mean, look at Tarantyev. He's always got some money-making scheme on the go. But he's still just a common clerk. I mean you have to admire his vulgar persistence but really he's just –

(HE'S NODDING OFF AGAIN WHEN ZAHAR RETURNS.

ZAHAR:	Mr Tarantyev's here!
OBLOMOV:	Let him in.
ZAHAR:	Are you sure?
OBLOMOV:	Of course I'm sure. Why ever not?
ZAHAR:	Because, sir – you'll forgive me from remarking – he'd sell his own granny for a pot of caviar.
OBLOMOV:	Zahar! Show him in.

BUT TARANTYEV, PUSHY AND
COARSE, BARGES IN ANYWAY.

TARANTYEV: Oblomov! How are you?
OBLOMOV: Thank you, Zahar. That will be all.
ZAHAR: (GLARING AT TARANTYEV) Suit
             yourself.

(ZAHAR LEAVES.)

TARANTYEV: Still stinking in bed, eh?
OBLOMOV: I was just getting up when you arrived! But
             I've been worrying over a problem. My
             landlord's asked me to move. What should I
             do? I like it here. The rooms are warm and
             dry and we've only been burgled once.
TARANTYEV: Don't worry, I can fix it for you. Just order
             some decent champagne for our dinner
             tonight and the problem's solved.
OBLOMOV: What do you mean?
TARANTYEV: Trust me. Now, first things first, you'll need
             to move to-morrow.
OBLOMOV: But –
TARANTYEV: Wait! Don't interrupt! You're moving to-
             morrow – to a flat on the Vyborg side. I
             know someone who's got one to let.
OBLOMOV: The Vyborg side! You must be joking. They
             say wolves come there in winter.
TARANTYEV: Alright, sometimes they run over from the
             islands – so bloody what?
OBLOMOV: It's so dull over there. Nobody who's
             anybody lives there.
TARANTYEV: Bollocks! My friend lives there. She's got a
             house of her own with a big kitchen garden.
             She's a widow with two children.
OBLOMOV: What's that to do with me? I'm not going .
TARANTYEV: What's your problem?
OBLOMOV: Well, for a start it's very central here. I'm
             right in the heart of St Petersburg. It's
             convenient for the shops, the theatres, my
             friends…

TARANTYEV: But you never go out! What's so important
             about being "central"?
OBLOMOV: Lots of things.
TARANTYEV: You don't even know yourself! What do
             you pay here?
OBLOMOV: Fifteen hundred roubles.
TARANTYEV: Well, over there you'd only be paying a
             grand for a whole bloody house nearly. I
             mean, look at this place! Quite frankly, it's a
             shit hole. You ought to be ashamed, a
             gentleman and landowner like yourself.
OBLOMOV: But I can't just move like that.
TARANTYEV: Why not? Look, consider it done. I'll go
             over and see the landlady and settle things.
             Then I'll be back in time for that champagne
             supper you've promised me.
OBLOMOV: But I don't want to move.
TARANTYEV: You'll thank me in the end. Just give me the
             money for the cab and I'll be off.
OBLOMOV: No, no, stop. Stop!

(IN HIS PANIC HE ALMOST GETS UP)

TARANTYEV: (LEAVING) Bye.
OBLOMOV: Stop! Stop! Listen!

(SUDDENLY HE FEELS SOMETHING
INSIDE THE BED. HE GASPS – AND
PULLS OUT A LETTER)

OBLOMOV: Oh, my goodness, that's where it was.
TARANTYEV: (STOPPING) Where what was?
OBLOMOV: The letter I've been looking for . From my
             bailiff in Oblomovka. It's was here all the
             time. How extraordinary!
TARANTYEV: What does it say?
OBLOMOV: (READING) "Sir, your honour, our father
             and benefactor, Ilya Ilyitch, dear master…"
TARANTYEV: Never mind all that!
OBLOMOV: (STILL READING) "The old people don't
             remember there ever having been such a
             drought, the spring crops are burned up as
             with fire. The winter crops have also been

9

ruined, some by caterpillars and some by early frosts...."

TARANTYEV: Who wrote this crap? Here – give it me.

OBLOMOV: No – wait. Here at the end after he's written that some of the peasants aren't paying their taxes and getting into arrears and others are simply running away. "I sent the wives to look for their husbands but the wives haven't come back either." Then he says (READING) "Sadly, this year we will be sending you some two thousand roubles less than last year, our father and benfactor. Unless, of course, the drought ruins us altogether. But we will do what we can."

TARANTYEV: Let me take a look!

(HE SNATCHES THE LETTER AND STARTS TO READ IT, GRUNTING INDIGNANTLY)

OBLOMOV: I wish I could remember what I received last year. I think it was seven or eight thousand. Stolz will remember. I'll ask him when he comes.

TARANTYEV: Bugger Stolz, this letter is lies from beginning to end.

OBLOMOV: You think so? Because I don't know how I can manage on only six thousand roubles!

TARANTYEV: This bailiff's taking the piss! I know for a fact that down at Shumilovo, the harvest was so good that all the debts were paid off. That's only thirty miles from your estate, so how come they did brilliantly and all your crops got burnt up in a drought?

OBLOMOV: (STARTLED) I don't know.

TARANTYEV: And all this talk about arrears! There shouldn't be any arrears if he was doing his job properly. And as for runaway peasants - I bet he's let them run off for a fat bribe!

OBLOMOV: What shall I do about it?

TARANTYEV: Sack the bastard!

OBLOMOV: Another bailiff might be even worse.

TARANTYEV: Then go down to Oblomovka and see for yourself.

OBLOMOV: But I've not been for twelve years!

TARANTYEV: Then it's about time you got off your arse and went.

OBLOMOV: I can't. Not before I've completed my plans for the improvement of the estate. They're still in draft form. Well, actually, they're still in my head so -

TARANTYEV: It's simple. Go down there for the summer and get that cheating bastard of a bailiff sorted. Then in the autumn come back to St. Petersburg and move into your splendid new flat.

(PAUSE)

OBLOMOV: But-

TARANTYEV: But what?

(PAUSE)

OBLOMOV: I mean – going down to the country! And moving into a new flat! I can't just rush into decisions like this. Can't you think of a compromise?

TARANTYEV: Don't be so bloody hopeless, Ilya Ilyitch! God knows what I could have done with my life if I'd had your advantages instead of sweating blood for every rouble.

OBLOMOV: I just wish Andrey was back. He'd sort this out in no time.

TARANTYEV: Stolz, you mean? He's nothing but a crook – and a German one at that.

OBLOMOV: (SUDDENLY SERIOUS) I'm sorry but you're talking about my best friend.

TARANTYEV: Best friend!

OBLOMOV: It's true. Andrey and I grew up together on neighbouring estates. We went to the same university and - anyway, he's only half German – on his father's side. His mother is Russian. He belongs to the Orthodox Church and Russian is his native tongue.

TARANTYEV:	If you keep going on about how bloody marvellous he is, I'm out of that door.
OBLOMOV:	You should respect him as my friend.
TARANTYEV:	Is that so? I mean, it's bad enough that his father comes over from Germany and makes shitloads of money. But the son has to go one better! He has to start minting money himself. Then he gets himself the rank of a court councillor. Then he decides to be some sort of intellectual and – (ULTIMATE INSULT) – travel!
OBLOMOV:	What's wrong with that?
TARANTYEV:	Would a Russian do that? A real Russian would do one job at a time and do it in his own good time. But not Stolz! It's not normal.
OBLOMOV:	Stop insulting him.
TARANTYEV:	Well, if he's so bloody wonderful, how come he wants to go ponceing about in foreign parts?
OBLOMOV:	To see things, to know about things, to study.
TARANTYEV:	It's all crap! Don't you trust him. He lies through his teeth – just like your bailiff.
OBLOMOV:	I do believe you're jealous.
TARANTYEV:	Don't be ridiculous! Oh, he may be very clever with his stocks and shares but I tell you -
OBLOMOV:	Mihey Andreyitch, you've made your point.
TARANTYEV:	Very well, I know when my advice is not wanted. Goodbye.
OBLOMOV:	Goodbye.

(PAUSE. TARANTYEV STARTS TO LEAVE)

TARANTYEV:	Oh, there is one thing –
OBLOMOV:	Yes?
TARANTYEV:	I'd forgotten. I'm off to a wedding to-morrow. Big posh affair. Could you lend me your dress-coat? Mine's a bit past it.
OBLOMOV:	It won't fit you.

TARANTYEV:	Course it will! Don't you remember? I tried on your frock-coat the other day. It could have been made for me. (CALLING) Zahar! Zahar! (PAUSE) He's not coming. You call him.
OBLOMOV:	(WITH A SIGH) Oh, very well! (CALLING VERY LOUDLY:) Zahar!

(ZAHAR APPEARS RELUCTANTLY)

ZAHAR:	What now?
OBLOMOV:	Will you bring me my dress-coat? Mikey Andreyitch wants to try it on. He's going to a wedding to-morrow.
ZAHAR:	Sorry, no.
TARANTYEV:	What do you mean – no?
OBLOMOV:	Explain yourself, Zahar.
ZAHAR:	Well, first of all, he ought to bring back the waistcoat and shirt he borrowed. They cost twenty five roubles and he's had them for five months.
TARANTYEV:	You heard your master.
ZAHAR:	I'm not giving you the dress-coat until you've brought all the other clothes you've borrowed back. Is that clear enough?

(PAUSE)

TARANTYEV:	Well, in that case – you can go to hell!
OBLOMOV:	But, Mikey Andreyitch –
TARANTYEV:	Oh, don't you worry, I'll rent you that flat whether you want me to or not.
OBLOMOV:	But –
TARANTYEV:	You'll be out on your ear here so you've got no choice, have you?
OBLOMOV:	But what's the hurry?
TARANTYEV:	Is or isn't it agreed?
OBLOMOV:	Well…
TARANTYEV:	Agreed or not?
OBLOMOV:	Oh, very well.
TARANTYEV:	And when I come back for supper - having solved all your problems – make sure

there's champagne. That's the deal. No ifs or buts.

(HE CHARGES OFF. A PAUSE.)

OBLOMOV: (WEARILY) Why is life so complicated?
ZAHAR: Search me. Maybe it's some sort of cosmic joke. I seem to remember you were on the point of getting up.
OBLOMOV: I was – before I was so rudely interrupted.
ZAHAR: (LEAVING) I await the miracle.

(LEFT ALONE, OBLOMOV YAWNS AGAIN)

OBLOMOV: It wasn't always like this, was it? When Stolz and I first came to St Petersburg back in – well, it must be twelve years ago – or maybe thirteen – or maybe eleven – I had some sort of career in the civil service mapped out. But I did so hate being ordered about. And women! I used to go to parties and meet them! I actually kissed a woman once. A woman who wasn't mother or nursey that is.

(ANOTHER YAWN)

But then you had to go through all those tedious parties and at homes and there'd be noise and chatter and – all for what? So I seem to have lost the habit. (DREAMILY) If only I could make Oblomovka like it used to be when I was a boy. When time seemed to last forever and the kitchen was full of delicious smells and the fields were full of contented cattle and…

(HE IS ABOUT TO DOZE OFF AGAIN WHEN THE DOCTOR BURSTS IN.)

DOCTOR: Ah, there you are, Ilya Ilyitch. Just as I thought!

14

OBLOMOV:	(STARTLED) Doctor, what's brought you here?
DOCTOR:	I've decided to come and see you because it's quite clear you're not going to come and see me. And as I was just down the road I thought I'd take the opportunity. (TAKING HIS HAND) Let's feel your pulse. Have you a cough?
OBLOMOV:	At nights. Especially after supper.
DOCTOR:	Hmm! How about palpitations? Headaches?
OBLOMOV:	Sometimes – yes.
DOCTOR:	I see.

(PAUSE. THE DOCTOR POURS HIMSELF A DRINK AND HELPS HIMSELF TO ANY AVAILABLE FOOD AS HE DELIVERS HIS JUDGMENT)

DOCTOR:	Well, if you ask my opinion –
OBLOMOV:	Of course, I do.
DOCTOR:	If you spend another two or three years in this climate, lying about and eating rich, heavy food, then you will die of a stroke.
OBLOMOV:	(AGHAST) You're sure?
DOCTOR:	I have no doubt whatsoever.
OBLOMOV:	So what am I supposed to do about it?
DOCTOR:	Do as other people in your situation do – go abroad.
OBLOMOV:	Abroad!
DOCTOR:	Yes. Somewhere warm and healthy. Why not?

(PAUSE)

OBLOMOV:	But, doctor – abroad!
DOCTOR:	What is there to prevent you?
OBLOMOV:	Everything.
DOCTOR:	What do you mean – everything?
OBLOMOV:	Well, for a start I haven't any money. I've had a letter from my bailiff which says –

(HE FUMBLES IN THE BED FOR THE LETTER)

OBLOMOV:	I'm sure I had it here a moment ago. (CALLING) Zahar! Zahar!
DOCTOR:	Look, that really doesn't matter. Your finances are your own affair. But it is my duty to tell you that you must change your way of life, your lodgings, the air you breathe, your occupation – everything. And above all –
OBLOMOV:	Yes?
DOCTOR:	Avoid worry.
OBLOMOV:	Avoid worry! I'm sorry, doctor, here I am with letters from my bailiff and notes to make on my ideas for –
DOCTOR:	That's another thing.
OBLOMOV:	What is?
DOCTOR:	You need to avoid thinking too much.
OBLOMOV:	But my plan of estate management is meant to –
DOCTOR:	My duty is merely to warn you. You must avoid strong emotions too. They hinder the cure. You must try and amuse yourself by riding, dancing, moderate exercise in the fresh air and, of course, pleasant conversation with the ladies –
OBLOMOV:	Well, that does sound a bit more promising.
DOCTOR:	Providing, of course, your emotions are stirred in a mild and pleasant way. No turbulent romance.
OBLOMOV:	Anything else?
DOCTOR:	You mustn't think for a moment about over-stimulating your brain with reading or writing. Instead, hire a dacha somewhere facing south and be sure to have women and song about you.
OBLOMOV:	How about wine?
DOCTOR:	Out of the question. Vodka would be even worse. As for food –
OBLOMOV:	Yes?
DOCTOR:	Avoid red meat, indeed I wouldn't recommend poultry either. Also anything floury or any sort of brawn or aspic. You can have lots of light soups and vegetables –

OBLOMOV:	Hurray!
DOCTOR:	Just remember there's cholera around so you'll have to be careful even then.
OBLOMOV:	Any other suggestions?
DOCTOR:	You should try and walk eight hours a day. Buy a gun so you have something to occupy yourself on the way.
OBLOMOV:	Good Lord!
DOCTOR:	Why not go to Paris for the winter? Amuse yourself there with the whirl of life.
OBLOMOV:	The whirl of life?
DOCTOR:	Go from a theatre to a dance or a fancy-dress ball or pay calls on friends. Enjoy – in moderation - laughter, women, music.
OBLOMOV:	(GETTING EXASPERATED) But no wine?
DOCTOR:	That goes without saying.
OBLOMOV:	(SAVAGELY) Anything else?

(PAUSE)

DOCTOR:	(SLOWLY) Well, perhaps you ought to try some sea air. Maybe you could get a steamer in England and take a trip to America.
OBLOMOV:	That's a good idea.
DOCTOR:	(STARTING TO LEAVE) Now if you carry out all this exactly –
OBLOMOV:	(SARCASTICALLY) Oh, every suggestion without fail –
DOCTOR:	If you do do that, then – I'm not promising, mind you – there is a chance that you may pull through. But if you carry on as you are – I'm not guaranteeing anything. All the best.

THE DOCTOR DISAPPEARS AS QUICKLY AS HE'D APPEARED. OBLOMOV GIVES A GROAN.

OBLOMOV:	Give me peace, just give me peace!

(THE GROAN TURNS TO A YAWN.

(HE SLUMPS BACK INTO SLEEP.
SUDDENLY THE CLOCK STRIKES
THREE AND HE AWAKES WITH A
START.)

OBLOMOV: Three o'clock! That can't be true! That bath'll be cold by now and there's really no point in getting into it. I'll tell Zahar to pour the water away,

(HE YAWNS. BUT HE IS RESTLESS)

OBLOMOV: Why do people batter your brain with suggestions? Change my flat. Move to the other side of St Petersburg. Go to my estate. Go abroad. Go to America! It's too much!

(HE GIVES A HEARTFELT SIGH)

OBLOMOV: Oh, I wish that Stolz was here.

(ON CUE ZAHAR APPEARS AGAIN.)

ZAHAR: You have another visitor.
OBLOMOV: Oh no!
ZAHAR: Andrey Ivanitch Stolz.
OBLOMOV: I don't believe it.

(STOLZ STRIDES VIGOROUSLY IN, A
SMILE ON HIS FACE.)

STOLZ: My dear friend!
OBLOMOV: Stolz! Stolz! You're back at last!
STOLZ: Of course.

(THE FRIENDS EMBRACE)

ZAHAR: I'll leave you to it.

(HE LEAVES.)

STOLZ: I can't believe you're still in bed.
OBLOMOV: Don't start, please.

STOLZ:	But I've been –
OBLOMOV:	Yes, I know, you've been up since dawn and all the way round the world since I last saw you.
STOLZ:	But what's to stop you travelling? You don't have to lie here like a lump of dough. You could be in Egypt in a fortnight and in America in three weeks.
OBLOMOV:	Andrey, I thought you were my friend!
STOLZ:	I am. You know I am.
OBLOMOV:	Then please don't be so quick with the recriminations. It's all very well for you to charge off all over the globe and look at things – and then come back and sort out your business affairs and then charge off again. But – I have to ask - why do you work so hard? What have you got to prove?
STOLZ:	Nothing. But work gives my life a completeness, a shape – and it suits me. I mean, it looks as if you've still banished work from your life and what's the result?
OBLOMOV:	That's not fair. I've got a great deal on my mind.
STOLZ:	You had when I left. And what have you done about it?
OBLOMOV:	Give me time – please.
STOLZ:	Do you go out anywhere?
OBLOMOV:	Now and then.
STOLZ:	Who visits you?
OBLOMOV:	You – the doctor – Tarantyev –
STOLZ:	That parasite! So what else do you do with your time?
OBLOMOV:	I read.
STOLZ:	What?
OBLOMOV:	(PRODUCING A BOOK FROM HIS BED) Well, for example, I'm reading this.
STOLZ:	(STUDYING IT) "A Journey to Africa"? Sounds interesting.
	(HE STARTS TO LOOK THROUGH THE BOOK.)
STOLZ:	Ilya, there's mildew in here.

OBLOMOV:	I did read the first couple of chapters. (PAUSE) When I first bought it.
STOLZ:	So – do you read newspapers instead?
OBLOMOV:	The print's too small.
STOLZ:	Ilyusha, you used to have interests, a social life, a job. What's happening?
OBLOMOV:	It just sort of crept up on me.
STOLZ:	Well, for God's sake, rouse yourself.
OBLOMOV:	I have tried. But then I think – why should I? What's the point?
STOLZ:	Listen - in two weeks I'm planning to go abroad again.
OBLOMOV:	All right for some!
STOLZ:	You could come with me.
OBLOMOV:	(A RAY OF HOPE) Could I?
STOLZ:	Why ever not?
OBLOMOV:	Indeed, why ever not.
STOLZ:	All you need to do is write the application for your passport then hand it in to-morrow!
OBLOMOV:	To-morrow! We need to think and talk about it – and then we'll see. Perhaps it's better if I go down to the country first – and go abroad afterwards.
STOLZ:	You know, Ilya, there are times when you seem too lazy to live.
OBLOMOV:	I think that's probably true.
STOLZ:	Well, I'm not going to leave you in this state. I'm taking you in hand.
OBLOMOV:	But, Andrey –
STOLZ:	(CALLING) Zahar! Zahar!

(ZAHAR ENTERS PROMPTLY)

ZAHAR:	Yes, Mr Stolz, sir.
STOLZ:	Get your master's clothes ready. He's going out.
OBLOMOV:	(IN PANIC) Andrey, please –
STOLZ:	Is there a problem, Zahar?
ZAHAR:	No, sir, it's just that I'll need time to polish his boots.
STOLZ:	Why aren't they already polished and waiting?

ZAHAR:	I did polish them last week but as the master didn't go out, they've grown dull and need polishing again.
STOLZ:	Get on with it!
ZAHAR:	(LEAVING) Very good, Mr Stolz, sir.

(PAUSE)

OBLOMOV:	But I can't go out like this. I haven't shaved.
STOLZ:	That's all right. I'll drive you to a barber's on the way.
OBLOMOV:	On the way where?
STOLZ:	To meet some friends of mine.
OBLOMOV:	You want me to – socialise?
STOLZ:	It's about time you did.
OBLOMOV:	But frenetic activity, the everlasting round of visits and invitations, the gossip, the backbiting, the way they look each other up and down -
STOLZ:	Ilya, these are good friends of mine. They're interesting, cultured people.
OBLOMOV:	I'm sorry they're all the same - dead behind the eyes, charging from one glittering event to another without rest or enjoyment. I mean, what sort of a life is that?

(PAUSE)

STOLZ:	(FIRMLY) Ilya, you seem very good at criticising other people. But what sort of life do you want for yourself?
OBLOMOV:	How can I say – with all the problems I'm facing and –
STOLZ:	All right, in an ideal world, what would you like?
OBLOMOV:	Ah, an ideal world. (HE SIGHS) Well, I would go to the country. With a wife, of course, so I'm not alone. And there would be good neighbours living nearby – you for instance. And when I get up in the morning, the weather would be lovely, the sky deep, deep blue without a trace of cloud. And while I waited for my wife to wake, I'd put

	on my dressing-gown and stroll in the garden to breathe the morning freshness. And – and I'd make a nosegay for her…
STOLZ:	Ilya, there's a bit of a poet in you.
OBLOMOV:	My wife, you see, wouldn't be the busy housekeeper sort of wife making preserves and measuring out yarn. She'd be cultured, well read, play the piano – and sing…

(SUDDENLY OUT OF NOWHERE THE VOICE OF A SOPRANO SINGING **CASTA DIVA** FROM BELLINI'S **NORMA**)

OBLOMOV:	(INSPIRED) Oh, yes, there'd be music. (SINGING ALONG) Casta diva…

(HE BREAKS OFF WHEN HE SEES STOLZ'S PUZZLED GAZE.)

OBLOMOV:	You see, it gets to me every time. Bellini's Norma. That poor proud druidess. (THE MUSIC RETURNS ANYWAY) What sorrows there are in those beautiful sounds! She's in love but there's nobody she can tell because she loves a Roman soldier and her father's a druid and so is everyone else around. Druids hate Romans and Romans hate druids so she has to keep her secret to herself. She is totally alone – and she sings to the moon…
STOLZ:	You should hear Olga Sergeyevna sing it!

(THE MUSIC RAPIDLY FADES)

OBLOMOV:	Who did you say?
STOLZ:	Olga Sergeyevna. She's one of the friends I want you to meet. I met her with her aunt in Switzerland.
OBLOMOV:	Her aunt?
STOLZ:	Yes, she's taken her under her wing. The parents are both dead. But, anyway, as I was saying, she has a wonderful voice.

OBLOMOV:	Olga or the aunt?
STOLZ:	Olga, of course. She's young and, well, maybe a bit unformed. A lot of people think she's difficult or stand-offish because she keeps herself to herself, doesn't gush rubbish, and doesn't suffer fools gladly. But I must admit I have a weakness for her.
OBLOMOV:	You mean…?
STOLZ:	Oh, good heavens, no! I don't mean in that way. She's far too young and immature! But she's still charming.
OBLOMOV:	I should like to meet her – sometime.
STOLZ:	Why not today? There's a party at her aunt's. That's where I'm going.
OBLOMOV:	But my clothes – my boots –
STOLZ:	(CALLING) Zahar! Zahar!
ZAHAR:	(ENTERING WITH SOME CLOTHES) Here, Mr Stolz, sir!
STOLZ:	Where are the boots?
ZAHAR:	I'm just bringing them

(HE GOES OUT)

STOLZ:	I'm sorry, Ilya, you've run out of excuses.
OBLOMOV:	But –
STOLZ:	No buts. It's time to get up.
OBLOMOV:	It's chilly.
STOLZ:	Then the sooner you get your clothes on.
OBLOMOV:	But my boots –
ZAHAR:	(RUSHING BACK IN) Here they are, master.
STOLZ:	Come on. You are getting up.
OBLOMOV:	(WITH EFFORT) I am getting up… I am getting up… I am getting up….

(PAUSE. HE THROWS OFF HIS
DRESSING GOWN. HE GETS OUT OF
HIS BED)

OBLOMOV:	(A NOTE OF WONDER) I'm up.

(TRIUMPHANT MUSIC.)

(THE MUSIC TURNS INTO THE
CHATTER OF A SMALL PARTY IN A
SMART DRAWING ROOM. FIGURES IN
THE BACKGROUND CHATTER AWAY.
OBLOMOV STAND THERE IN HIS
BEST CLOTHES DAZED BUT
EXCITED.)
(OUT OF THE BACKGROUND STOLZ
EMERGES WITH A YOUNG WOMAN
ON HIS ARM. THIS IS OLGA – BRIGHT,
ATTRACTIVE, SELF-CONTAINED,
UNCONVENTIONAL.)

STOLZ: Olga Sergeyevna, may I present my dear friend, Ilya Ilyitch Oblomov?

OLGA: How do you do?

OBLOMOV: I – I'm well. How do you do?

OLGA: I've heard so much about you from Andrey.

OBLOMOV: I – (SUDDENLY ALARMED) What's he told you?

OLGA: Nothing but good things of course. About how you grew up together and studied together and -

OBLOMOV: So he hasn't told you anything about now?

STOLZ: Ilya, relax. Olga is about to sing for us.

OBLOMOV: What are you going to sing?

OLGA: Casta diva. From Bellini's Norma. Do you know it?

OBLOMOV: (SOFTLY) Oh yes, I know it.

STOLZ: Olga Sergeyevna, your pianist awaits.

OLGA: (TO OBLOMOV) If you know the piece, then I'd value your opinion of my performance. Be honest – please. You never learn how to improve if all you hear is flattery.

OBLOMOV: Of course, of course. But really – I know nothing.

(STOLZ LEADS OLGA AWAY
TOWARDS AN EXPECTANT GROUP.
OBLOMOV SEATS HIMSELF IN
ANXIOUS ANTICIPATION)

(AN EXPECTANT HUSH. THEN OLGA –
A DISTANT FIGURE IN THE
BACKGROUND - STARTS TO SING
CASTA DIVA ACCOMPANIED ONLY
BY A PIANO.)
(OBLOMOV LISTENS INTENTLY)

OBLOMOV: Yes, Stolz was right. She's got a fine voice.
(LISTENING) Ahhh.....heaven! It's so
powerful, so moving. It's almost too much
for a sensitive soul. I do hope I don't cry...

(THE SINGING CONTINUES THEN -)

OBLOMOV: (A NOTE OF PANIC) I do believe she's
looking at me – yes. Perhaps I've put on odd
stockings – or my shirt's inside out. If that's
the case, I'll murder Zahar.

(THE SINGING CONTINUES)

OBLOMOV: No, she's definitely looking. As if somehow
I'm interesting – or there's a spot on the end
of my nose. Maybe she thought because I
shut my eyes to appreciate the music that I'd
fallen asleep. Oh, I hope not. Phew! She's
looking away.

(THE SINGING CONTINUES)

OBLOMOV: And now she's looking back. I expect she
realises that I alone appreciate her singing.
Or maybe she's just checking to see that I
haven't closed my eyes again.
(THOUGHTFULLY) I mean, if I was being
honest, she's not a beauty in the strict sense
of the word. She's tall and calm and – oh –
those wonderful wide-awake, blue-grey
eyes! They shine with the light of intelligent
thought.

(THE SINGING IS NEARING ITS
CONCLUSION)

OBLOMOV:	(AGHAST) Oh my God, I do believe I may be falling in love!
	(POLITE APPLAUSE AS THE SINGING ENDS) (OBLOMOV RISES FROM HIS SEAT. LIGHTS CHANGE. HE IS WITH STOLZ AND OLGA THOUGH STILL IN A DAZE.)
STOLZ:	No, I mean it, that was delightful, Olga.
OBLOMOV:	More than delightful.
OLGA:	Thank you. I fear I went a little flat in the opening. It is very difficult to sing.
OBLOMOV:	No, no, you were perfect –
STOLZ:	You were certainly good.
OLGA:	Good will do. Oh, Andrey, I'm so glad that you're back in St Petersburg.
STOLZ:	For the moment.
OLGA:	What do you mean?
STOLZ:	I'm off abroad again – the usual mixture of business and pleasure.
OLGA:	He's hardly ever here, is he, Mr Oblomov? It's not fair on his friends, is it?
OBLOMOV:	I agree - but Andrey's always enjoyed gadding about all over the world.
STOLZ:	Yes, and this time Ilya's coming with me.
OLGA:	Are you?
OBLOMOV:	I – I'm joining him later. Once I've sorted out my business affairs. And – and some other important things I need to do.
OLGA:	So you're a business man too?
OBLOMOV:	No – not exactly. But I do have an estate to run and –
STOLZ:	You're not backing out of it this time, Ilya.
OLGA:	All the same, Andrey, I do think it's unfair of you to go away again so soon. And to take your friend, whom I've only just met, with you. There are so very few interesting people in St Petersburg.
OBLOMOV:	You – you find most of them superficial?
OLGA:	Oh yes. Don't you?

26

OBLOMOV:	As a matter of fact, I do.
STOLZ:	We'll be back soon, don't you worry.
OLGA:	I should like to travel.
OBLOMOV:	Would you? Well, yes, I suppose there's a lot to be said for it when you think about it. Broadening the mind and that sort of thing.
STOLZ:	I shall remind you of those words, Ilya.
OLGA:	Anyway, Andrey, if you are going away so soon, you must come and talk to my aunt. She'll be very cross if you go away again without chatting to her. Are you coming, Ilya Ilyitch?
OBLOMOV:	Should I?
STOLZ:	Olga's aunt is a most sophisticated and intelligent woman.
OBLOMOV:	No, I mean, I didn't want to intrude.
OLGA:	She'd love to meet you. (MATTER-OF-FACT) What a pity you're going abroad so soon as well.
OBLOMOV:	I suppose I could always reconsider. There are a lot of practical problems, passports and luggage and -
STOLZ:	(FIRMLY) Ilya, I'm not going to let you get out of this. I'm leaving in a fortnight and you are joining me within a week. Is that agreed?
OBLOMOV:	Yes, of course. But –
STOLZ:	Promise?
OBLOMOV:	I promise.
OLGA:	Now do come and meet my aunt.

(OLGA'S AUNT ADVANCES FROM THE BACKGROUND TO GREET THEM. OBLOMOV FOLLOWS THE OTHERS TO MEET HER STILL IN A DAZE. (BLACKOUT. THE SOUNDS OF SOMEONE SINGING **CASTA DIVA**.) (THE SINGING FADES AWAY TO BE REPLACED BY THE COUNTRY MUSIC FROM THE START.) (LIGHTS UP ON A LUSH COUNTRY SETTING)

(OBLOMOV IS SITTING IN A ROCKING
CHAIR IN HIS DRESSING GOWN – OR
PERHAPS HIS BED HAS BEEN
ADAPTED AND RE-DRESSED FOR THE
COUNTRYSIDE.
THE MUSIC FADES.
OBLOMOV SIGHS CONTENTEDLY.)

OBLOMOV: Well, it really is extraordinary how things
turn out! Thank goodness Stolz got me out
of bed. If he hadn't got me out of bed then I
would never have met Olga Sergeyevna and
her aunt. And if I hadn't started dining with
them then I'd never have heard about this
delightful dacha close to the one they
always hire for the summer. And without
their encouragement I would never have
found the energy to hire it – without even
looking at it. And now I have looked at it, I
have to say that I love it. And I feel as if
I've lived here for ever. It's so calm and so
peaceful and… (ANOTHER YAWN) ...and
so unlike St Petersburg. Truly this has been
a remarkable few weeks. I'm here with Olga
from morning to night. I read to her, I send
her flowers, I go walking with her, I go
boating on the lake. All because I heard her
singing 'Casta diva!

(PAUSE)

OBLOMOV: What my feelings for her are, well, time
alone will tell. No need to rush. Best to just
relax and enjoy the good things in life.

(HE STARTS TO HUM **CASTA DIVA**
THEN BREAKS OFF)

OBLOMOV: I suppose I have rather let poor old Stolz
down. He did sound a bit cross in his last
letter but I do think being abroad would be
terribly exhausting. Like being at a big party
in St Petersburg only worse because you

28

literally can't understand a word anybody's saying because they're all foreign. Oh no, this is the life.

(HE YAWNS. THEN STARTS TO SNORE.)
(OLGA APPEARS, DRESSED FOR WALKING)

OLGA: (BRIGHTLY) Mr Oblomov! Mr Oblomov!

(HE AWAKES WITH A START)

OLBOMOV: What?
OLGA: I thought for a moment you'd dozed off.
OBLOMOV: No, no, of course not. I always close my eyes when I'm thinking hard.
OLGA: Are you ready for our walk?
OBLOMOV: (DECISIVELY) Yes, of course. (GETTING UP WITH SURPRISING ALACRITY) Shall we go?

OBLOMOV THROWS OFF HIS DRESSING GOWN AND OFFERS HIS ARM TO OLGA)
(THEY WALK OFF INTO THE GREEN OF THE COUNTRY.)
(THE SOUNDS OF NATURE LOUDER NOW.)
(AT FIRST THEY WALK IN SILENCE.)
(FINALLY OLGA SPEAKS)

OLGA: So you've had a letter from Andrey Ivanitch?
OBLOMOV: Yes.
OLGA: What does he say?
OBLOMOV: He's still urging me to meet up with him in Paris.
OLGA: And will you?
OBLOMOV: Well, I suppose I'll go eventually.
OLGA: When?
OBLOMOV: As soon as I'm ready. I don't really know.
OLGA: (DISMAYED) But you do intend to go?

OBLOMOV:	I don't want to let Andrey down. I did promise I'd join him as soon as I could. All the same I -
OLGA:	(CUTTING IN) Don't you like it here?
OBLOMOV:	I like it here very much.
OLGA:	There's nothing wrong with your dacha?
OBLOMOV:	Nothing at all.
OLGA:	Then why on earth do you want to go?
OBLOMOV:	I don't really.
OLGA:	I'm beginning to wonder if it's me you can't stand.
OBLOMOV:	Don't be absurd. (QUICKLY CHANGING SUBJECT) Oh look – there are some lilies of the valley, let me pick some for you.

(HE PICKS SOME FLOWERS)

OBLOMOV:	There!
OLGA:	Thank you.
OBLOMOV:	They're still wet with dew. I love lilies of the valley. They smell of nature and fields and woods.
OLGA:	So you're not a fan of roses?
OBLOMOV:	Oh no, the scent's far too strong. In fact, flowers are all very well in the fields but indoors they're just too much trouble. And when they die, they make such a mess.
OLGA:	(DRYLY) Yes, I've heard how fussy you are about keeping your rooms clean.
OBLOMOV:	It's Zahar's fault. He just won't do the job properly.
OLGA:	Then you ought to employ someone who does.

(PAUSE)

OBLOMOV:	Shall we walk on?

(THEY CONTINUE WALKING)

OLGA:	When you go abroad, will you go straight to Paris?

OBLOMOV:	I don't know. It's where Andrey is. Why do you ask?
OLGA:	I wanted you to take a letter to him. It'll be quicker than the mail – if you're going soon, that is.
OBLOMOV:	Well, I ought to be. I just haven't set a date yet.
OLGA:	Are you so very unhappy here?
OBLOMOV:	Olga – that's the second time – have I upset you in some way?
OLGA:	No, why do you ask?
OBLOMOV:	It's just that, well, you seem angry with me.
OLGA:	And why do you think that is?

(SHE STOPS WALKING. SHE LOOKS HIM FULL IN THE FACE)

OLGA:	You must have some idea.
OBLOMOV:	Well, yes, I suppose. (CLEARING HIS THROAT) The fact is – Olga Sergeyevna – I have feelings –
OLGA:	Feelings?
OBLOMOV:	Yes, for you. Of course, the way you sing "Casta diva" has something to do with it. But not I think everything. What I mean to say is – the last thing in the world I'd want to do is upset you. Because – you're important to me. And I'd hate you to be angry with me.
OLGA:	It's you that's saying I'm angry.
OBLOMOV:	But – you are, aren't you?
OLGA:	Don't be ridiculous. I am nothing of the sort. And I do really think it's time I went home.

(SHE STARTS TO WALK SWIFTLY AWAY)

OBLOMOV:	(RUNNING AFTER HER) Olga – stop!
OLGA:	(STOPPING) What is it now?
OBLOMOV:	That's the wrong way. This way's quicker.
OLGA:	Oh, very well.

31

(THEY WALK IN THE DIRECTION
OBLOMOV HAS INDICATED. SILENCE.
FINALLY -)

OBLOMOV: Please – forgive me -
OLGA: But it really isn't polite to insist you can't
            wait to get away from here.
OBLOMOV: But that wasn't what I said! It certainly
            wasn't what I meant. The fact is –
OLGA: What?
OBLOMOV: No, I'm afraid to say it. You'll get cross
            with me again.
OLGA: Please – say it.
OBLOMOV: It's just that – when I look at you like this, I
            – I feel very close to tears. You see, I've no
            pride. I'm not ashamed of my feelings.
OLGA: But why do I make you want to cry?
OBLOMOV: That's difficult to say. I know I'm not the
            most decisive of men. But bringing feeling
            from in here to out there – if you know what
            I mean – is so very hard. I'm sorry.
OLGA: Mr Oblomov – I forgive you.

(SHE OFFERS HER HAND. HE KISSES
IT)

OBLOMOV: Thank you, oh, thank you.
OLGA: I just wish that once, just once –
OBLOMOV: Yes?
OLGA: You could tell me what you're really
            thinking. And now I must get back before
            my aunt starts worrying. Thank you for the
            flowers. Goodbye.

(SHE RUNS OFF.)

OBLOMOV: Well, a fine mess you made of that, Ilya
            Illyitch! And yet – I don't think I've got it
            completely wrong. She does seem to care
            for me. When I think of how she looked at
            me just now when I gave her the lilies of the
            valley! (PAUSE) I'm just being a coward. I
            could ask her to marry me and then –

(FIRED WITH ENTHUSIASM, HE
STARTS WALKING BACK
ENERGETICALLY HOME.)

OBLOMOV: Yes, why not? When I go abroad I could
             take her with me. We'd go to the Italians
             Lakes, we'd walk among the ruins in Rome,
             we'd ride in a gondola in Venice, get lost in
             a crowd in Paris and London and then – yes
             - I'd take her back to my earthly paradise.
             My Oblomovka.

             (HIS ROCKING CHAIR COMES BACK
             INTO VIEW.
             STILL TALKING OBLOMOV SITS ON
             IT AND STARTS TO ROCK HIMSELF.)

OBLOMOV: Yes, yes, I just know they'd all adore her
             there with her lovely face and her sensitive
             eyes and her fine, slender neck. They won't
             have seen anything like her. They'll fall at
             the angel's feet. And we will –

             (HE SUDDENLY STOPS ROCKING)

OBLOMOV: What on earth am I thinking! I'm imagining
             the whole thing. She can't love an absurd
             creature like me – with sleepy eyes and
             flabby cheeks. And yet – where's that
             mirror?

             (HE LOCATES A MIRROR LYING
             AMONG THE PILE OF POSSESSIONS
             SCATTERED ROUND HIS CHAIR)
             (HE STUDIES HIMSELF)

OBLOMOV: Well, there's no doubt I look better than I
             used to do when I was in town. My eyes are
             brighter and that stye seems to have cleared
             up completely. And my skin's pinker. No
             doubt because of all the fresh air I've been
             breathing – and the walks – and the fact that

I'm drinking less. Perhaps Olga's not so crazy... if she does love me, that is. Well, at the very least I'm not going to need to go abroad as the doctor insists. Not in a hurry anyway. And never if I'm not in the mood.

(ZAHAR APPEARS, CLEARING HIS THROAT)

ZAHAR: Excuse me, master –
OBLOMOV: What is the matter?
ZAHAR: You've got an invitation to a supper party.
OBLOMOV: Where?
ZAHAR: Where do you think?
OBLOMOV: Olga's aunt, of course.
ZAHAR: Do you want me to accept then?
OBLOMOV: Of course, I want you to accept, you fool!

(BLACKOUT. SOMEONE SINGING A PLANGENT RUSSIAN FOLK SONG)
(LIGHTS UP. OLGA IS IN THE BACKGROUND SINGING.)
(OBLOMOV SITS WITH OLGA'S AUNT, A PLEASANT, WORLDLY-WISE WOMAN.)

AUNT: I'm so glad that you could join us, Ilya Ilyitch.
OBLOMOV: And I'm delighted to be here, believe me.
AUNT: I know you always enjoy Olga's singing.
OBLOMOV: She has a fine voice.
AUNT: But I hope you will permit me to take the opportunity - while she is otherwise engaged – to have a little word with you.
OBLOMOV: Of – of course.

(OLGA'S SINGING CONTINUES)

AUNT: Now I am neither blind nor stupid and it is clear to me that the two of you are very taken with each other.
OBLOMOV: I'm not sure I am worthy to aspire to Olga –

AUNT:	To be frank, I'm not sure either. But I think you are a good, kind and intelligent man so I am prepared to be convinced.
OBLOMOV:	(DOWNCAST) I see. Of course.
AUNT:	The fact is that you have become something of a project for my dear Olga. She believes that she will be able to reform you.
OBLOMOV:	Reform me? You mean –
AUNT:	I mean – she intends to make you shake off your lazy ways and fulfil your full potential. She is convinced that you are a jewel of great price that needs only polishing to sparkle.
OBLOMOV:	I had no idea.
AUNT:	Oh, I'm sure you had. Olga is a very bright and determined girl. She's always been an individualist with her own views on how things should and should not be. If anybody's going to reform you, it's Olga.
OBLOMOV:	Of course, but –
AUNT:	I do hope I'm not alarming you.
OBLOMOV:	Not in the least. All the same –
AUNT:	All the same what?
OBLOMOV:	I don't want to disappoint her.
AUNT:	I'm sure you don't. Anymore than I want you to disappoint her. Because there is another consideration –
OBLOMOV:	Which is?
AUNT:	Olga is still young and while I myself am very liberal and accommodating in these matters, there are those who would say it is not entirely proper for a young unmarried girl to spend so much time alone with an older unmarried man.
OBLOMOV:	Oh no, that had never occurred to me.
AUNT:	Of course, there has been no suggestion of impropriety and these are after all the relaxed ways of the country not the rigid social rules of St Petersburg.
OBLOMOV:	But I am bringing her into disrepute, is that what you're saying?
AUNT:`	Ilya Ilyitch, please.

OBLOMOV:	But I am. The poor deluded girl thinks that she can make a worthless creature like myself less worthless. And for this fatal error of judgement, she will pay a terrible social cost.
AUNT:	You are jumping to conclusions.
OBLOMOV:	No, I see it all. (GETTING UP) I must save Olga Sergeyevna from her own generous, over trusting nature. I am not worthy of her, really I am not.
AUNT:	Ilya Ilyitch, do sit down please.
OBLOMOV:	I cannot delay. I must save her.

(HE STARTS TO WALK AWAY)

AUNT:	Ilya Ilyitch, come back, come back!

(BUT HE'S ALREADY GONE)
(UNWARE, OLGA KEEPS ON SINGING.)
(THE SINGING FADES. BLACKOUT.)
(LIGHTS UP ON OBLOMOV IN HIS ROCKING CHAIR FRANTICALLY WRITING A LETTER.)

OBLOMOV:	"My dear Olga Sergeyevna, you will be surprised to receive this letter when we have been seeing each other so often. But please read it to the end and you will see that I could not have acted differently. Although I should have started off by writing it and so saved both of us a great deal of trouble and remorse."

(PAUSE)

This is hard. The hardest letter I've ever written – or failed to write.(HE SIGHS) But it has to be done.

(HE CONTINUES WRITING)

OBLOMOV: "The fact is - we fell in love with each other so quickly and so unexpectedly that it was like suddenly falling ill. Which is why it's taken me so long to recover."
(SCRATCHING WITH PEN) No, I can't say that, it's plain rude. (WRITING CONTINUES) "After all, who - having looked at you and listened to you for hours on end – could voluntarily undertake the hard task of breaking the spell?"

(A SIGH. THEN ALMOST CHEERFUL:)

OBLOMOV: That's more like it! (WRITING) "Every day I've thought 'I will stop where I am, I won't lead you on.' But I got carried away and only now have I succeeded in looking deeper into the abyss into which I am falling. I speak only of myself, of course. You will be soaring high above it like an angel of purity."

(PAUSE.)

OBLOMOV: (FIRMLY) "Listen I will say it simply and clearly – without beating about the bush. You don't love me, you can't love me and really it's much the best thing for you that you don't. Trust me. We have reached the stage when love becomes a disease. You've become restless, thoughtful, your nerves are unstrung. And so I say we must stop before your position becomes intolerable. In a few weeks it will be impossible. Love makes such incredible progress it's like a galloping gangrene of the soul." (PAUSE) That's very good. But – am I mad, am I really doing this? (PAUSE) Yes, I am! (THE WRITING CONTINUES) "Many people will wonder why I am running away like this but I am prepared for that. It will be a slight comfort to me in my deep anguish to think that this short episode of our lives will leave such a

pure and fragrant memory that, as far as I
am concerned, it will be enough to prevent
me from sinking once more into spiritual
slumber. While – for you, it will serve as a
guide to real love in the future…"

(PAUSE)

OBLOMOV: (TEARFULLY) "Good-bye, my angel, and
make haste and fly away – as a frightened
bird flies from a branch it has settled on by
mistake. Good-bye… Goodbye…."

(HE STOPS WRITING)

OBLOMOV: I'm exhausted. (CALLING) Zahar! Zahar!
ZAHAR: (ENTERING) What is it now?
OBLOMOV: I want to make sure this gets to Olga
Sergeyevna as soon as possible. Before she
goes for her walk.
ZAHAR: What is it?
OBLOMOV: It's a letter! What does it look like?
ZAHAR: I'll get the maid to run over with it.
OBLOMOV: At once, you understand, at once!
ZAHAR: (GRUMBLING) At once, at once! Not like
you to be in such a hurry.
OBLOMOV: Don't be impertinent – just do it!
ZAHAR: (EXITING) All right, all right, keep your
hair on.

(PAUSE. OBLOMOV ROCKS
CONTENTEDLY IN HIS CHAIR.)

OBLOMOV: Well, that's that over. A great deal of
embarrassment saved on all sides. She'll get
my letter and she'll read it and she'll…
(SUDDEN HORROR) Oh, my God, what
have I done?

(HE LEAPS TO HIS FEET)

OBLOMOV: Zahar! Zahar!

OBLOMOV: I have to get to her before – before she reads it.

(HE RUNS OFF.)
(THE LIGHTS CHANGE TO
COUNTRYSIDE AS HE FINALLY
STOPS, PANTING AND EXHAUSTED)

OBLOMOV: It's no use. I've no breath left. The maid will have got there ages ago. (HE SEES SOMETHING) Oh, my God, there she is!

(HE ATTEMPTS TO HIDE BEHIND A
SMALL PIECE OF FOLIAGE.)
(OLGA ENTERS)

OLGA: I can see you there, Ilya Ilyitch, there's no point in hiding.
OBLOMOV: (EMERGING) I wasn't hiding.
OLGA: Then what were you doing?
OBLOMOV: I – I was sparing your feelings.
OLGA: Well, don't bother – please. Here – take it.

(SHE OFFERS THE LETTER TO HIM)

OBLOMOV: I was – er – wondering if you'd read it.
OLGA: As much as I could before bursting into tears. (GETTING TEARFUL) Go on – take it. Before I start crying all over again.

(SHE STARTS TO CRY IN EARNEST)

OBLOMOV: I – I'd do anything not to make you cry!
OLGA: How can you say that? Go on – you have made me cry. Make the most of it.
OBLOMOV: But – I was doing it all for the best.
OLGA: Oh yes, you seem very convinced that we'd be better of without each other. And I've been trying so hard not to lose hope. Not to believe that you would never do anything useful, never change your ways, never

	declare your love. It serves me right for my pride.
OBLOMOV:	But I do love you. That's why –
OLGA:	If you ask me, you prefer your dressing-gown to me.
OBLOMOV:	(HURT) That's unfair!
OLGA:	So why did you write that our love was a terrible mistake – like, what was it?
OBLOMOV:	(SHAME-FACED) A galloping gangrene.
OLGA:	How could you?
OBLOMOV:	I didn't mean it literally, I meant that –
OLGA:	You were better off without me.
OBLOMOV:	No, you were better off without me,
OLGA:	What's the difference in the end? Oh, and I was feeling so happy.

(SHE STARTS CRYING AGAIN)

OBLOMOV:	Olga, please – I have been torturing myself.
OLGA:	What's the good of that? You talk about falling into an abyss and torturing yourself and getting galloping gangrene and then you ask me to believe that you are a sweet and gentle human being. The terrible thing is that you are a sweet and gentle human being. You just haven't got the least idea of how to behave. (BIG EFFORT) Good-bye, Ilya Ilyitch.

(SHE STARTS TO RUN OFF)

OBLOMOV:	(RUNNING AFTER) Olga, please – stop.

(THEY COME TO A BREATHLESS HALT)

OLGA:	I'm sorry, Ilya, but I've had enough! I can't take any more of this endless hesitation and delay. One moment I think I know what you feel and the next moment you're saying something else. You invent problems when there aren't any problems there.
OBLOMOV:	You really think there aren't?

OLGA:	It's clear to me that you love me.
OBLOMOV:	Which is why I wanted to spare you.
OLGA:	And I love you.
OBLOMOV:	Well, if you say so.
OLGA:	(FIRMLY) I love you.
OBLOMOV:	That's wonderful, that's magnificent. But –
OLGA:	But what?
OBLOMOV:	If we go on meeting like this, your position is going to be compromised.
OLGA:	What do you mean?
OBLOMOV:	Well, according to your aunt, tongues are wagging.
OLGA:	It doesn't bother me or my aunt. Why should it bother you?
OBLOMOV:	Well, because I care for you and –
OLGA:	Besides, there's a very simple solution.
OBLOMOV:	Which is?
OLGA:	You ask me to marry you. Then we'll be properly engaged and it'll be all right.
OBLOMOV:	(GULP) I – ask – you – to –
OLGA:	To marry you, exactly! Well?

(PAUSE)

OBLOMOV:	Olga Sergeyevna – will you marry me?
OLGA:	Of course.
OBLOMOV:	And now – may I kiss you?
OLGA:	Of course. (A BIG KISS) There!
OBLOMOV:	I can't believe it! Life is delightful! Life is simple! I am free – quite free – to do whatever I want. Come on, kiss me again. My – my bride to be!

(THEY KISS AGAIN)

END OF ACT ONE

ACT TWO

(OBLOMOV SITS COMPOSING A
LETTER. COUNTRY SOUNDS AROUND
HIM)

OBLOMOV: "My dear Andrey, thank you so much for
your letter. 'Now or never' you say,
repeating your kind invitation to join you in
Switzerland and then proceed to Italy. Of
course, it would be wonderful to be gadding
about the world as you are. But the fact is –
I have some momentous news. I have
become engaged to Olga Sergeyevna…"

(PAUSE. A SIGH OF RELIEF)

OBLOMOV: There! I've said it now. Told him in black
and white that Olga and I are to be wed!
After all, it's only fair, he introduced us and
so – no, no, it's too soon to let everybody in
on our secret and have them interfering and
demanding to know our plans. Particularly
Stolz who's hundreds of miles away….

(HE SCREWS UP THE PAPER AND
STARTS AGAIN)

OBLOMOV: (WRITING) "My dear Andrey, of course I
would love to join you in Switzerland but
life is never that simple. You have been
urging me for some time to visit my estate
at Oblomovka, sort out my affairs, rouse the
peasants to work and ascertain what my
income actually is. Excellent advice so, of
course, that has to be my first priority.. But
before I can go there, I have to complete my
plans for the reformation of the estate. Plans
which still need to be put down on paper
and…"

(PAUSE. HE SIGHS.)

43

OBLOMOV:	It doesn't sound good. Perhaps it is best if I just tell him about the engagement. He should be the first one to know. (STARTING AGAIN) "My dear Andrey..."

(ZAHAR APPROACHES)

OBLOMOV:	(BREAKING OFF) What is it, Zahar? Can't you see I'm writing a letter?
ZAHAR:	You've got a visitor, master.
OBLOMOV:	Oh?
ZAHAR:	Mr Tarantyev. He's come down from St Petersburg specially to see you. The thieving swine!
OBLOMOV:	Zahar – please.
ZAHAR:	I'll show him in. But if he wants to borrow a dinner suit, tell him to bring back all the other clothes he's pinched from you.

(TARANTYEV BUSTLES IN.)

TARANTYEV:	Oblomov! How are you?
OBLOMOV:	(POINTEDLY) That will be all, Zahar.
ZAHAR:	(LEAVING) Don't say I didn't warn you.

(OBLOMOV OFFERS TARANTYEV A SEAT)

OBLOMOV:	I must say, Mikey Andreyitch, it's very good of you to come and see me.
TARANTYEV:	No problem. The fact is – I wondered when you were going to come and take a look at your lovely new flat on the Vyborg side.
OBLOMOV:	(DISMAYED) Ah, I -
TARANTYEV:	After all, I did spend a great deal of time and energy arranging that flat for you when you got chucked out of your old one. Even went to the bother of transporting all your possessions over there.
OBLOMOV:	My dear Tarantyev, I'm really sorry. But I don't need the flat any more.
TARANTYEV:	Oh?
OBLOMOV:	I'm not going to live there.

TARANTYEV:	What are you talking about?
OBLOMOV:	I don't need it.
TARANTYEV:	You've obviously forgotten about the contract.
OBLOMOV:	What contract?
TARANTYEV:	The contract you've signed for a year.
OBLOMOV:	When?
TARANTYEV:	Just before you charged off down here. Of course, you can just give me eight hundred roubles and I'll settle up with the landlady and that'll be the end of it.
OBLOMOV:	Eight hundred roubles! I've no recollection of this contract. And if I did sign it, I most certainly didn't read it.
TARANTYEV:	The more fool you!
OBLOMOV:	Besides, there's a very good chance I'll be going abroad soon.
TARANTYEV:	Oh you're always talking about going abroad.
OBLOMOV:	But I've bought the portmanteau!
TARANTYEV:	(SAVAGELY) Big deal! Listen – why don't you just hand me the six months' rent in advance you've agreed to. That's only four hundred roubles.
OBLOMOV:	I won't be rushed. I'll come over one day soon – when I'm back in St Petersburg – and make arrangements to sub-let this wretched flat. Will that do?
TARANTYEV:	How do you know it's a wretched flat? You've not seen it!
OBLOMOV:	I don't want to see it. It's in the Vyborg district. It's too far from -
TARANTYEV:	From what?
OBLOMOV:	From the centre of town.
TARANTYEV:	Why does that matter? You just lie in bed all day.
OBLOMOV:	Not any more!
TARANTYEV:	How come?
OBLOMOV:	Because –
TARANTYEV:	Because what?
OBLOMOV:	(HOTLY) It's none of your business.

TARANTYEV: Very well then. Are you going to give me
              the money now or not? The contract's cast-
              iron.
OBLOMOV: I dare say it is. But I haven't got any
              money!
TARANTYEV: (RISING) Well, it seems I've made this
              journey on a bloody fool's errand. The least
              you can do is pay for my cab down here.
OBLOMOV: How much was it?
TARANTYEV: Ten roubles.
OBLOMOV: Ten roubles! That's outrageous! (WITH A
              SIGH) Oh, very well. Here.

              (HE HANDS OVER THE MONEY)

TARANTYEV: And then there's my dinner.
OBLOMOV: What about your dinner?
TARANTYEV: I'll be back in town too late to eat so I'm
              bound to have to stop at some expensive
              pothouse on the way. Say another five
              roubles.
OBLOMOV: (SIGHING) Oh very well.

              (MORE MONEY IS HANDED OVER)

OBLOMOV: (CALLING) Zahar! Mr Tarantyev is going!
ZAHAR: (CALLING BACK) Well, ask him why he
              hasn't brought back the shirt and waistcoat
              he borrowed months ago!
TARANTYEV: (MUTTERING) You know, Oblomov, you
              should sack that foul-mouthed old shitbag of
              a servant. (LOUDLY) I'll see myself out.
ZAHAR: (FROM AFAR) A wise decision!

              (TARANTYEV STARTS TO LEAVE
              THEN RETURNS)

TARANTYEV: You know, I really do advise you to come
              and see this flat. I think you'll like it.
OBLOMOV: Yes, yes, now will you please go? I have an
              important social engagement.
TARANTYEV: You've an engagement?

46

OBLOMOV: (FIRMLY) Yes – and – and – it's none of
               your business.
TARANTYEV: No need to take that tone!

               (HE LEAVES. OBLOMOV GETS UP
               AND PUTS ON HIS OVERCOAT.

OBLOMOV: Mustn't be late.

               BLACKOUT. THE SOUNDS OF THE
               COUNTRY LOUDER NOW.
               LIGHTS UP ON OBLOMOV AND OLGA
               WALKING IN THE COUNTRYSIDE.)

OLGA: I shall hate it when the cold weather comes
               and we'll have to head back to town.
OBLOMOV: Me too. I'm a different person here.
               (ANXIOUSLY) I have changed, haven't I?
OLGA: Immensely.
OBLOMOV: All because of you.
OLGA: I never doubted that you could do it if you
               really wanted to.
OBLOMOV: You know, I was writing to Stolz to explain
               why I wasn't joining him in Switzerland and
               I wanted so much to tell him of our
               engagement –
OLGA: (CONCERNED) But you didn't?
OBLOMOV: Of course not.
OLGA: It's far too soon.
OBLOMOV: Usually it's me who's in favour of putting
               things off.
OLGA: It's not putting them off. It's making sure
               we do everything in the right order. You'll
               have to go down to Oblomovka first.
OBLOMOV: It's a good idea but –
OLGA: Ilya, before she'll accept you as my fiancé,
               my aunt will have to know what sort of
               income you have.
OBLOMOV: Precious little at the moment.
OLGA: That's why you must visit your estate and
               start making reforms.
OBLOMOV: Stolz has suggested that I must have a
               proper house built, then make a road, then

	open schools. It's enough work for a lifetime.
OLGA:	You've already been drawing up plans for the improvements, haven't you?
OBLOMOV:	Yes, but –
OLGA:	Ilya, please finish them and go.
OBLOMOV:	Maybe we could go there together.
OLGA:	And where would we stay? Is there a house there?
OBLOMOV:	Sot of. The old house was practically falling apart the last time I saw it twelve years ago.
OLGA:	Twelve years! That's terrible!
OBLOMOV:	I know.
OLGA:	We must find a flat in town in the meantime.
OBLOMOV:	Well, I have a flat there of sorts. But it's really not suitable.
OLGA:	Then find another!
OBLOMOV:	(DISTRESSED) Olga, stop, please stop!
OLGA:	What's the matter?
OBLOMOV:	We ought to be enjoying the sweet anticipation of the wonderful life we're going to have together. We ought to be dreaming of things we can enjoy together. Instead it's – go to the courts, go to Oblomovka, find us a flat. You're as bad as Stolz! Why do we have to be in such a hurry?
OLGA:	We have to deal with the practicalities. You ought to go to St Petersburg as soon as you can. Get rid of this flat.
OBLOMOV:	Yes, yes, yes! I just wish –
OLGA:	What?
OBLOMOV:	Everything didn't have to be done in a rush.
OLGA:	Ilya, please -
OBLOMOV:	We've been so happy here in the country. It's going to be hard going back to the hustle and bustle of the city.
OLGA:	(SOFTLY) Ilya, do you love me?
OBLOMOV:	Oh yes, of course.

(THEY KISS)

OLGA:	Then please do the things I ask. I know you can if you try.
OBLOMOV:	I will, I promise but –
OLGA:	Winter will soon be here. We'll be back in St Petersburg then.
OBLOMOV:	But –
OLGA:	Go, my love – please…

(BLACKOUT. THE SOUNDS OF BUSY
CITY STREETS)
(CHILDREN PLAYING AND
GIGGLING)
(LIGHTS ON AGAFYA BUSY
SWEEPING THE FLOOR.)
(SHE STOPS FOR A MOMENT)

AGAFYA:	Quiet, children, quiet. You'll wake Mr Oblomov!

(AS SHE LEAVES STILL SWEEPING,
THE LIGHTS COME UPON OBLOMOV.
HE'S BACK AMIDST CLUTTER AND
DISARRAY IN A DISHEVELLED BED.
HE GIVES A CONTENTED YAWN)

OBLOMOV:	It's strange how well life can work out if you don't hurry too much. When I got back to town, I came and looked at this flat and, well, it's on the small side but it's really not that bad. And my belongings were already stored here so it would have been a tremendous bother moving them all out again. (PAUSE) And really – despite what I thought - Vyborg's not such a bad area.

AGAFYA ENTERS. SHE COUGHS
POLITELY

AGAFYA:	Excuse me, Mr Oblomov –
OBLOMOV:	What is it, Agafya Matveyevna?
AGAFYA:	I don't want to bother you but I wondered if you might like me to make you some coffee.
OBLOMOV:	That's very kind of you.

AGAFYA:	Well, it's just that I noticed that Zahar doesn't make it properly. He adds too much chicory and doesn't boil it enough. So I thought –
OBLOMOV:	Thank you, Agafya Matveyevna, that would be delightful.

(AGAFYA LEAVES)

OBLOMOV:	And then there's the landlady. She's a simple soul but really very pleasant. Salt of the earth. Admirable in her way. She's lost her husband and brought up two children on her own. And she looks after her mother who's an invalid with swollen legs. And the children are very well behaved most of the time. (YAWNS) Oh yes, one could definitely have done worse. Quite where Tarantyev fits into all this I've no idea but if the money I've given him keeps the landlady happy and I like the flat then it's ridiculous to worry.

(ZAHAR ENTERS WITH SOME COFFEE.)

OBLOMOV:	That was quick!
ZAHAR:	I didn't make it.
OBLOMOV:	I know.
ZAHAR:	And she says she's baking a pie.
OBLOMOV:	Oh? Just simple peasant fare I expect – carrots and onions.
ZAHAR:	No, as good as anything we ever had at Oblomovka with chicken and fresh mushrooms.
OBLOMOV:	That sounds good!
ZAHAR:	So do you want some?
OBLOMOV:	Yes, please.
ZAHAR:	(EXITING) I'll tell her. God knows how that crook, Tarantyev, ever found you a decent berth like this.
OBLOMOV:	That's quite enough, Zahar.

ZAHAR:	Knowing that bastard, there's bound to be a nasty surprise sooner or later. So best make the most of it. Before disaster strikes.

(PAUSE. ZAHAR RETURNS)

ZAHAR:	Oh, I forgot to tell you.
OBLOMOV:	What?
ZAHAR:	A servant came from Olga Sergeyevna's aunt. They're expecting you at the opera tonight.
OBLOMOV:	Oh, my goodness, I'd forgotten all about it!
ZAHAR:	So – are you going?
OBLOMOV:	(DEFENSIVELY) Of course! It's Bellini's Norma and Casta Diva is my favourite. Olga Sergeyevna sings it beautifully.
ZAHAR:	When's the wedding going to be? After Christmas?
OBLOMOV:	What wedding?
ZAHAR:	Yours, of course!
OBLOMOV:	Whatever gave you that idea?
ZAHAR:	Oh, come on, master, I'm not that daft. Everybody's talking about it.
OBLOMOV:	So who's everybody? I mean, Olga is the soul of discretion and –
ZAHAR:	And?
OBLOMOV:	Nothing's set in stone. Anyway, who's spreading these rumours?
ZAHAR:	Katya told Semyon, Semyon told Nikita, Nikita told Vassilissa, Vassilissa told Anissya and Anissya told me.
OBLOMOV:	Oh my God!
ZAHAR:	I don't see what your problem is. What's the big deal about getting married? People are doing it all the time.
OBLOMOV:	I am not just "people"! Besides, you don't understand what it means. You suddenly cease to be yourself and become "a bridegroom". Public property. And people come up to you and say the most stupid things by way of congratulations. And there's fuss about what you're going to wear and what you're going to eat and who's

51

	going to be invited. It's a complete nightmare.
ZAHAR:	Sorry I raised the subject.
OBLOMOV:	So you should be.
ZAHAR:	Then if anybody asks me about whether you're getting married to Olga Sergeyevna, shall I just say the whole thing is a pack of lies?
OBLOMOV:	Yes! (PAUSE) No!
ZAHAR:	You were all over her in the country.
OBLOMOV:	That's none of your business!
ZAHAR:	You were though.
OBLOMOV:	In the country there was just the two of us. In town we both lead busy social lives.
ZAHAR:	Well she does anyway.
OBLOMOV:	I really don't want you or anybody else drawing any conclusions.
ZAHAR:	I thought you were engaged.
OBLOMOV:	Who told you that?
ZAHAR:	You did - in the first flush of enthusiasm.
OBLOMOV:	Well, we are – in a manner of speaking. But it's very much a private matter.
ZAHAR:	So you won't be joining her at the opera then?
OBLOMOV:	That's not what I said.
ZAHAR:	So you will be joining her at the opera?
OBLOMOV:	No! (PAUSE) Yes!
	(BLACKOUT. THE ORCHESTRAL INTRODUCTION TO ACT ONE OF BELLINI'S **NORMA**.) (THE MUSIC FADES) (LOUD APPLAUSE. THEN AUDIENCE INTERVAL CHATTER IN A FASHIONABLE OPERA HOUSE) (LIGHTS UP. THE INTERVAL CHATTER CONTINUES) (IN THE FOREGROUND OLGA TALKS TO OBLOMOV)
OLGA:	I'm so glad you came!
OBLOMOV:	Of course, I've come.
OLGA:	I was beginning to worry.

OBLOMOV:	I wanted to see you so I've come – that's all.
OLGA:	It's just that now we're back in St Petersburg, we don't see each other anything like as much as we used to. I've missed you.
OBLOMOV:	Well, that's city life for you, isn't it? (AGITATED) Oh, I can't bear it!
OLGA:	Whatever's the matter?
OBLOMOV:	Who are all these people? They all keep staring at us.
OLGA:	Don't be absurd!
OBLOMOV:	I'm not imagining things. I heard them as I was arriving. Two over-dressed young men lounging by the staircase. One of them said "Who's that fellow?" And the other said: "Somebody by the name of Oblomov." "What's he doing here?" "Oh, he's just a friend of Stolz's."
OLGA:	Does it matter?
OBLOMOV:	But – "somebody by the name of Oblomov". Is that what it's come to?
OLGA:	You're worrying about nothing.
OBLOMOV:	I'm sorry but I just don't feel comfortable. You know I've never liked all this noise and bustle and chatter –

NICOLAI, A SWAGGERING MILITARY DANDY, APPROACHES.

NICOLAI:	Olga Sergeyevna –
OBLOMOV:	(SOTTOVOCE) That's it! I'm going!
OLGA:	Come back. (TO NICOLAI) If you'll excuse us for a moment.
NICOLAI:	(KNOWINGLY) Of course, I didn't mean to intrude. (RETREATING) We'll talk later.
OBLOMOV:	Look at him, just look at him.
OLGA:	What are you talking about?
OBLOMOV:	He's smirking, positively smirking. As if he's in on some big joke. As if he knows everything about us.
OLGA:	You are going down to Oblomovka soon, aren't you?

OBLOMOV:	When my plans are ready, yes. But I'm having difficulties deciding the curriculum for this school I'm going to build in the village. It's not easy to decide whether to teach domestic economy to all the children or just the girls. (PAUSE) That friend of yours, Nicolai, is definitely staring.
OLGA:	He's a friend of my aunt's.
NICOLAI:	(CALLING FROM AFAR) Olga Sergeyevna – please. Don't let Mr Oblomov monopolise you the whole interval.

(THE INTERVAL CHATTER
CONTINUES)

OBLOMOV:	I'm sorry but I really can't stay here any longer.
OLGA:	What are you talking about? You adore opera.
OBLOMOV:	I do, particularly Bellini. Don't forget that hearing you sing "Casta diva" first made me love you.
OLGA:	Oh, Ilya, I'm so relieved to hear you say that!
OBLOMOV:	But you know how much I love you.
OLGA:	Yes, but I do sometimes worry that maybe you're sliding back into your old ways.
OBLOMOV:	Nonsense! It's just that coming here and hearing some fat soprano sing the aria just isn't the same.
OLGA:	I thought she sang it beautifully.
OBLOMOV:	Yes, I'm sure she did.
OLGA:	You're not ill?
OBLOMOV:	No, no, I'm well and happy.
OLGA:	Well, you certainly seem to have settled in to your new flat very easily. It was worrying you a great deal before you moved in.
OBLOMOV:	It doesn't worry me now. I'm more adaptable than you might think.
OLGA:	Perhaps I should come and visit you there.
OBLOMOV:	I don't think you'd like it.
OLGA:	Why ever not?

OBLOMOV:	It's not smart in the way you're used to.
OLGA:	Suddenly you've got a very grand idea of the life I lead.

(THE BUZZ OF CONVERSATION STARTS TO FADE)
(IN THE DISTANCE THE ORCHESTRA CAN BE HEARD TUNING)

OLGA:	The second act's about to start. We should go back in. My aunt will be worried.
OBLOMOV:	I'm not sure that I can.
OLGA:	Why ever not?
OBLOMOV:	We're deceiving people – particularly your aunt. She's a smart woman. She suspects something. They all do.
OLGA:	But -
OBLOMOV:	No, you're young. You don't know the world and how cruel it can be. You believe in the purity of our love so much that it never enters your head the trouble we're heaping upon ourselves.
OLGA:	Ilya, I may be young but I am not naive. The trouble's all of your own making. All you have to do is what you promised to do.
OBLOMOV:	Yes, yes, but your aunt might start asking about my income before I've fully prepared the answers.
OLGA:	None of this worries me.
OBLOMOV:	You're very brave. That's because you don't understand the way in which your reputation will be affected by the drip drip drip of rumour.
NICOLAI:	(CALLING) We're going in now, Olga!

(HE DISAPPEARS BACK INTO THE THEATRE)

OLGA:	(UPSET) Are you coming?
OBLOMOV:	I've upset you!
OLGA:	(BRAVE) No, not at all.
OBLOMOV:	I can see it in your face.
OLGA:	I'm not upset.

OBLOMOV: Yes, you are. All because of my stupidity
             and insensitivity.

             (THE MUSIC OF THE PRELUDE TO
             ACT TWO OF **NORMA** BEGINS)

OLGA: Come on – you know you'll enjoy it.
OBLOMOV: No, no, give my regards to your aunt – and
             Nicolai or whatever his name is – and – say
             – say that I'm not feeling very well.
OLGA: Where are you going?
OBLOMOV: Home.
OLGA: (TIGHTLY) Very well. If that's what you
             want. But don't forget next Wednesday.
OBLOMOV: What about next Wednesday?
OLGA: My aunt has an at home.
OBLOMOV: (LEAVING) I'll be there I promise!
             Goodbye, Olga.

             (HE KISSES HER. THEN HURRIES
             AWAY

OLGA: (CALLING AFTER HIM) Goodbye, Ilya.

             (THE MUSIC CONTINUES TO BUILDS.)
             (OLGA STANDS THERE FOR A
             MOMENT

OLGA: (SOFTLY) I do still love you. And
             sometimes I wish I didn't.

             (WITH AN EFFORT SHE TURNS AND
             MAKES HER WAY BACK INTO THE
             THEATRE.)
             (THE MUSIC GRADUALLY FADES)
             (LIGHTS UP)
             (OBLOMOV IS LYING IN BED)
             (HE IS LOST IN THOUGHT)
             (AGAFYA ENTERS CARRYING A
             LARGE CLOTHES BASKET)

AGAFYA: I've begun sorting out your socks, Mr
             Oblomov.

OBLOMOV:	That's very kind.
AGAFYA:	Shall I put them down here on the chair?
OBLOMOV:	Yes, yes, of course. Do you need any help?
AGAFYA:	No, no, I'll be fine.

(SHE PUTS THE BASKET DOWN AND
CONTINUES SORTING AS THEY
TALK.)

OBLOMOV:	Do you mind if I ask you something?
AGAFYA:	Not at all. Ask away!
OBLOMOV:	Mr Tarantyev –
AGAFYA:	What about him?
OBLOMOV:	He – he manages your affairs for you?
AGAFYA:	Oh yes. He takes care of everything and gives me enough to run the household.
OBLOMOV:	So Mr Tarantyev –
AGAFYA:	Yes?
OBLOMOV:	Well, I'm sorry if I seem intrusive or nosy but – I don't understand – what exactly is Mr Tarantyev's place in your life?
AGAFYA:	(CALMLY) He's my brother. I thought you knew that.
OBLOMOV:	Your brother? Yes, of course, of course.

(THE SORTING CONTINUES)

AGAFYA:	Well, you have fifty-five pairs of socks in all –
OBLOMOV:	Really? I'd no idea.
AGAFYA:	But most of them are in holes.
OBLOMOV:	You shouldn't trouble yourself.
AGAFYA:	Don't be silly. It's my job to look after things. You have no one else to see to it and I enjoy doing it so where's the problem?
OBLOMOV:	Still, I'm not sure you should -

(SHE RUMMAGES IN THE BASKET)

AGAFYA:	Twenty pairs are no good. They're not even worth darning.
OBLOMOV:	Then by all means throw them away!
AGAFYA:	(SHOCKED) Throw them away!

OBLOMOV:	I can always buy new ones. I can't bear you wasting your time on stuff like this!
AGAFYA:	Why ever not? These ones can be re-heeled easily. And these…

(MORE RUMMAGING IN THE BASKET)

OBLOMOV:	At least if you're going to sort them, do sit down.
AGAFYA:	No, no, thank you. I haven't time! It's my washing day and I have to get the clothes ready.
OBLOMOV:	Don't you ever stop?
AGAFYA:	(RUMMAGING) There's always something to be done. The children need feeding or their clothes need washing or I have to do some shopping for my mother.
OBLOMOV:	But - don't you get tired?
AGAFYA:	Well, I don't mind admitting I sleep like a log once my head hits the pillow. But that's natural, isn't it? And then next morning I'm up bright and early to start another day.
OBLOMOV:	(HALF TO HIMSELF) Extraordinary! Quite extraordinary!
AGAFYA:	So – do you want me to re-heel these socks? I can order some yarn. An old woman brings it to us from the country. It isn't worth buying what they sell here in town, it's such poor stuff.
OBLOMOV:	This is very kind of you. Only I really am ashamed of your taking all this trouble.
AGAFYA:	Not at all, I'm happy to oblige. You see, these ones I'll re-heel myself, these I'll give to Granny and then tomorrow my sister-in-law is coming to stay with us.
OBLOMOV:	So that's Mr Tarantyev's –
AGAFYA:	Heavens, no! Who'd marry him? It's my other brother's wife. And while she's here we'll have nothing to do in the evenings so we'll refoot them then. My little Masha is learning to darn too.
OBLOMOV:	Does she like it?

AGAFYA:	Well, these needles are a bit big for her to handle just now but she's getting the hang of it.

(SHE PICKS UP THE BASKET.)

AGAFYA:	So that's agreed then.
OBLOMOV:	I – I really don't know how to thank you. I'm very much obliged to you – and to Masha. Perhaps I could buy her a silk frock by way of a present.
AGAFYA:	(BASKET IN HANDS) I wouldn't hear of it, Mr Oblomov! What does Masha want with silk frocks? It's job enough to provide her with cotton ones. She wears her things out in no time – especially her shoes. We can't buy them fast enough. And now –

(SHE STARTS TO MOVE AWAY)

OBLOMOV:	No – please –
AGAFYA:	I'm afraid I have to get started on the washing. Maybe another time you could come and take coffee with us.
OBLOMOV:	Yes, I'd like that.
AGAFYA:	Perhaps when my brother drops in.
OBLOMOV:	Is he here very often then?
AGAFYA:	Every time the money needs sorting out.
OBLOMOV:	I see. So why exactly -
AGAFYA:	(LEAVING) I really ought to get going.
OBLOMOV:	Of course. I won't detain you.

(PAUSE. THEN SHE STOPS AND REACHES DOWN AGAIN INTO THE CLOTHES BASKET

AGAFYA:	Oh, I forgot to say. I've taken your dressing-gown out of the store-room. (PRODUCING IT) It's easily washed and mended.
OBLOMOV:	There's no need!
AGAFYA:	The stuff is very good! It could serve you for years!

OBLOMOV: But I don't wear it any more! I've given it
              up! (MORE FERVENTLY) The days of
              sitting around in a dressing-gown are over!
              And they are not coming back!

AGAFYA: Well, it still won't do any harm to have it
              washed. Perhaps you'll start wearing it
              again – when you're married!

              (SHE PICKS UP THE BASKET AND
              LEAVES.)
              (OBLOMOV SIGHS.)

OBLOMOV: Oh my God, she knows about the
              engagement too! I mean if Agafya
              Matveyevna, who is the gentlest and most
              benign of creatures knows, then everyone
              knows. And Olga wonders why I flinch at
              the scrutiny of society.

              (HE PRODUCES A LETTER FROM THE
              BEDCLOTHES)

OBLOMOV: Poor dear Olga! She does sound so very
              upset. What on earth made her fall in love
              with me? Why do I keep on loving her when
              I know how bad it is for her? And what sort
              of love is it? Nothing but anxiety and
              agitation! A fear of being misunderstood or
              understood too well! (PAUSE) You know, I
              really was enjoying that conversation about
              my socks. It's such a pity Agafya had to
              spoil it by mentioning the wedding. But –

              (HE STARTS SEARCHING FOR PEN
              AND PAPER)

OBLOMOV: I must write to Olga! I – I really can't face
              going to her aunt's. I'll say I'm ill.

              (ZAHAR ENTERS WARMING
              HIMSELF.)

ZAHAR: It's bloody freezing out there.

OBLOMOV:	(INDIGNANTLY) Zahar, language!
ZAHAR:	Pardon me, master, but the weather's cold enough to freeze your bollocks off.
OBLOMOV:	Zahar, please –
ZAHAR:	Well, it wasn't me who wanted to go across the river to buy some sweets for the landlady's children, was it? As I recall, it was you.
OBLOMOV:	What is your point, Zahar?
ZAHAR:	I've had a lousy journey home. The Neva's on the point on icing over and I've had a hell of a job finding a boatman to row me across.
OBLOMOV:	The river's icing over?
ZAHAR:	Yes – all the bridges have been removed.
OBLOMOV:	You mean it'll be impossible to get into town?
ZAHAR:	Well, if you hurried you might just make it.
OBLOMOV:	And if you didn't hurry?
ZAHAR:	You'll be stuck here in Vyborg till the ice melts.
OBLOMOV:	(SIGH OF RELIEF) Thank goodness for that.

(LIGHTS CHANGE. AGAFYA
SWEEPING AS USUAL.)
(OBLOMOV IN BED WRITING.)

AGAFYA:	I'll make your coffee, Mr Oblomov. As soon as I've finished sweeping up.
OBLOMOV:	There's no rush.
AGAFYA:	But I know how much you like your coffee. And I've baked a sugar-loaf to go with it.
OBLOMOV:	Delicious! You know, you ought to remarry. You look after the house so splendidly.
AGAFYA:	Who'd marry me with my two children? As my brother never stops reminding me.

(SHE LEAVES. OBLOMOV RETURNS
TO HIS LETTER.)

OBLOMOV:	(WRITING) "My dear Olga, I am so sorry to have missed your aunt's Wednesday

soirée. My cold continues to be as bad as ever. Thank heavens that the ice is finally beginning to melt and it was possible for your loyal Nikita to bring over your dear letter and the books which…" (PAUSE) "which of course I intend to get down to reading just as soon as I have finalised my plans for Oblomovka and arranged to go down there."

(PAUSE)

OBLOMOV: Well, I have read fifteen pages of one of them already so that's hardly a lie. (WRITING) "Zahar tells me the bridges have been fixed so, my dear, provided that my cold continues to improve, I will be with you very soon."

(HE SIGHS)

OBLOMOV: Why are these things always so hard to write?

(ZAHAR BURSTS IN)

ZAHAR: You've got a visitor, master.
OBLOMOV: I'm busy.
ZAHAR: She's told me to make myself scarce.
OBLOMOV: She?
ZAHAR: Olga Sergeyevna, of course.
OBLOMOV: (IN PANIC, HIDING HIS LETTER) Oh my goodness, I don't believe it. Get out of here at once, Zahar.
ZAHAR: But I've only just come in.
OBLOMOV: Go to the market and get us something for supper.
ZAHAR: Anything in particular?
OBLOMOV: No! Just go there very fast and come back here very slowly and –

(OLGA COMES IN)

OLGA:	(EMBRACING HIM) Ilya!
ZAHAR:	Don't mind me, I'm off.

(HE LEAVES.)

OBLOMOV:	You're alone?
OLGA:	No, no, my maid's waiting below.
OBLOMOV:	But still – you're here alone – in my room. Your reputation -
OLGA:	My aunt's away for the day so nobody's going to find out. Besides, I had to come.
OBLOMOV:	(SLOWLY) So you've managed somehow to get across the river.
OLGA:	It wasn't that difficult. All the bridges are back in place. Apparently they've been back for some time.

(AWKWARD PAUSE)

OBLOMOV:	Well, of course, if I'd been well enough but –

(HE TRIES AN UNCONVINCING BURST OF COUGHING)

OBLOMOV:	I've had this terrible cold. It's better now. But not better enough for me to get out and about, of course. And then there's my sore throat -
OLGA:	It doesn't sound like you've got a sore throat.
OBLOMOV:	Doesn't it? (ATTEMPTING SORE THROAT) It keeps coming and going, you see. And then just as -
OLGA:	(CUTTING IN) Ilya, you have deceived me.
OBLOMOV:	But, Olga, I –
OLGA:	Why?

(PAUSE)

OBLOMOV:	I was afraid.
OLGA:	What of?
OBLOMOV:	Talk, gossip.

OLGA:	You're not still fretting about that?
OBLOMOV:	But even the servants know!
OLGA:	Although you weren't afraid of me not being able to sleep at night and nearly falling ill with worry?
OBLOMOV:	Of course I was worried about that!

(PAUSE)

OLGA:	In that case, why don't you do something so that you can talk directly to my aunt and get all this uncertainty over with?
OBLOMOV:	It's not that easy, is it? Your aunt is bound to want to ask me lots of questions about my finances.
OLGA:	So why you still not managed to get any answers?
OBLOMOV:	I – I've written, I really have, but I still haven't received a reply.
OLGA:	You're not going down to Oblomovka?
OBLOMOV:	All in good time,
OLGA:	Ilya – I'm not sure I understand you any more.
OBLOMOV:	Oh – please! Don't say that!
OLGA:	At least you could have written and told me what was going on instead of talking about the bridges and the cold.
OBLOMOV:	I wanted to spare you –
OLGA:	(FIRMLY) Ilya, I am not a child.
OBLOMOV:	But you are young and –
OLGA:	I may be younger than you but I repeat – I am not a child. The fact is – I am losing hope!
OBLOMOV:	Please don't do that!
OLGA:	Then help me! I mean, what do you do all day? This is not a nice flat, Ilya. The ceilings are low, the windows are small, the wallpaper's peeling.
OBLOMOV:	(DEFENSIVELY) I'm sorry but I'm very settled here.
OLGA:	So – how do you spend your time?
OBLOMOV:	Oh, reading, writing, thinking about you –

OLGA:	What did you make of that book I sent you about Catherine the Great?
OBLOMOV:	I – I found it very interesting.
OLGA:	You haven't looked at it, have you?
OBLOMOV:	I did glance at it.

(OLGA LOOKS AT HIM PITYINGLY)

OLGA:	And what about your plans to reform Oblomovka?
OBLOMOV:	I have so little time. When I get up in the morning, they're tidying the rooms and disturbing me. Then the conversations about what we're having for dinner begin and the landlady's children come in and ask me to help them with their homework. And after dinner –
OLGA:	You sleep.
OBLOMOV:	Yes.
OLGA:	Why?
OBLOMOV:	So as not to notice the time. Life is so dull and unendurable when you're not around.
OLGA:	Ilya, do you remember that day in the country when you asked me to marry you and said you suddenly felt free? You remember how you took me by the hand and said I was yours – and how I gave you my consent?
OBLOMOV:	Of course! How could I forget? It's transformed my whole life.
OLGA:	(SADLY) No, it hasn't.
OBLOMOV:	You know that if you needed my life, I would gladly die for you.
OLGA:	What would be the point of that? Why can't you just do what you need to do?
OBLOMOV:	But without you, I am nothing!
OLGA:	Then why do you drive me mad with your indecision? I've seen other people when they're in love. It isn't like this. They are active and full of life. They don't hang their heads, their eyes are wide open. They don't go to sleep, they act!
OBLOMOV:	(SOFTLY) Oh, Olga!

OLGA:	What is it?
OBLOMOV:	You are magnificent! You are no longer a child! You have become a woman, a proud, beautiful, intelligent, clear-sighted woman!
OLGA:	Ilya, are you listening to what I'm saying?
OBLOMOV:	Of course. When you are not here, there is a danger that I sink into lethargy and sleep. But now you are here – I have risen from the dead. I am inspired!
OLGA:	Oh, Ilya, I do hope that is true. You are such a good man and I hate to see you wasting yourself.
OBLOMOV:	So do I! I promise I'll reform! I will sort out my estate, I will go down there in person, I will see the authorities about our wedding. I will talk to your aunt and –
OLGA:	Please – don't promise what you cannot perform!
OBLOMOV:	But in your presence, I am released and I can.
OLGA:	Ilya, this is your last chance. I have to go now but you must give me your word that you will come and see me soon at my aunt's. I have made this journey once and it's up to you to make the next. Do you understand?
OBLOMOV:	Oh yes, my love, of course.

(HE KISSES HER)

OBLOMOV:	You don't mind?
OLGA:	Why should I?
OBLOMOV:	Oh, how glad I am you came here, Olga.
OLGA:	(MOVED) So am I.

(ANOTHER KISS)

OLGA:	And now I really must go. Don't fail me, Ilya.
OBLOMOV:	I promise. Goodbye, my love.
OLGA:	Goodbye.
OBLOMOV:	Safe journey!
OLGA:	Ilya, the bridges are perfectly safe now.

(SHE LEAVES. AS SHE GOES, SHE
PASSES AGAFYA SWEEPING THE
FLOOR OUTSIDE. THEY STOP AND
STARE AT EACH FOR A MOMENT.
THEN OLGA DEPARTS AND AGAFYA
RETURNS TO HER SWEEPING)
(MEANWHILE OBLOMOV IS ON A
HIGH)

OBLOMOV: Yes! Yes! Yes! I can remember now the
             way it used to be. Suddenly I know I can
             recover the excitement and the energy – and
             the love…

             (ZAHAR RETURNS)

ZAHAR: So she's gone already?
OBLOMOV: It's no concern of yours.
ZAHAR: I wasted as much time as I could. And I
             bought some asparagus.
OBLOMOV: I hate asparagus!
ZAHAR: Good. I'll eat it instead.

             (HE PRODUCES A CRUMPLED
             LETTER)

ZAHAR: The landlady gave me this. Came for you
             while you were otherwise occupied, if you
             know what I mean.
OBLOMOV: It's from Oblomovka. From my neighbour!
ZAHAR: The one you asked to keep an eye on
             things?
OBLOMOV: (STIFFLY) Really, Zahar, that is none of
             your business.
ZAHAR: (EXITING) Anything rather than visit the
             bloody place.

             (OBLOMOV OPENS THE LETTER AND
             STARTS TO READ)

OBLOMOV: "Dear Ilya Ilyitch, I earnestly beg you to
             entrust the care of your estate to someone

                              67

else. The responsibility is beyond me. To be
honest, it would be best if you came here
yourself and better still if you settled here. It
is a fine estate but it is badly neglected. In
the present state of things you are not likely
to receive more than three thousand
roubles…" (PAUSE) Only three thousand,
what will Olga's aunt say?

(HE SKIMS THROUGH THE LETTER.)

OBLOMOV: "Your house is in a very bad way. I've
advised your servants to move out because
it's no longer safe. Please –make haste and
come…"

(PAUSE. HE PUTS DOWN THE LETTER)

OBLOMOV: So what do I do now? It's worse than last
year! So much for rediscovered energy!
There's no choice. The marriage will have
to be postponed. And I'll have to find an
architect to repair the house and in the
meantime, what? A loan? But what if I can't
pay it in time? I'll be in an even worse
mess. Maybe I could mortgage the estate.
But that's just as bad except that's there no
getting out of it. And by the end of it there
might not be enough left to live on!

(A SIGH)

OBLOMOV: I only wish Stolz was here or at least
someone with a practical mind!

(A SUDDEN THOUGHT. HE CALLS
OUT)

OBLOMOV: Agafya Metveyevna! Agafya Metveyevna!
AGAFYA: (COMING IN) Yes, Mr Oblomov.
OBLOMOV: Will you ask your brother to come and see
me?

(LIGHTS CHANGE)
(TARANTYEV SITS WITH OBLOMOV
WITH THE LETTER IN HIS HAND.)

TARANTYEV: Well, you're in the shit and no mistake. Still, it's only twelve hundred miles and in another week the roads will be fit for sleighing.

OBLOMOV: But I'm out of the habit of travelling. Particularly in winter.

TARANTYEV: So how many peasants do you having paying you tax?

OBLOMOV: I've no idea.

TARANTYEV: Well, then, how much tax do they pay?

OBLOMOV: I don't know. (PLAINTIVELY) Listen, I don't know anything about peasants' work or how you tell whether a peasant is considered rich or poor. I don't know what a quarter of rye or oats means, when they sow and reap it or how they sell what they reap. The fact is – I don't know anything!

TARANTYEV: Which is why you've come back to me?

OBLOMOV: Yes. As Stolz is still away and –

TARANTYEV: Oh, you're always throwing Stolz in my face! A fat lot of gratitude I've had for finding you this fantastic apartment.

OBLOMOV: Belonging to your sister.

TARANTYEV: Don't you like her?

OBLOMOV: Very much – but you might have mentioned she was your sister. After all, you did insist on that contract and some people have said to me –

TARANTYEV: (RISING) Well, if it's like that, I'm off.

OBLOMOV: No, no, please, don't!

TARANTYEV: The next thing I know you'll be belly-aching about clothes I've borrowed.

OBLOMOV: But you've never returned them.

TARANTYEV: Right. That's it.

(HE MAKES TO LEAVE.)

OBLOMOV: Tarantyev – please! I apologise!

TARANTYEV: Oh, very well. I'll let you take advantage of
               my better nature.

(HE SITS AGAIN)

TARANTYEV: Particularly as I do have a suggestion.
OBLOMOV: Ah!
TARANTYEV: Basically you need to hand the estate over to
               a man who understands farming.
OBLOMOV: Exactly!
TARANTYEV: You get the deed of trust transferred to him
               instead of your neighbour.
OBLOMOV: Yes – but where do I find such a man?
TARANTYEV: (IMPRESSIVELY) Isay Fomitch Zatyorty.
OBLOMOV: He's a friend –
TARANTYEV: A sometime colleague. He's a smart guy,
               experienced and business-like. Except for
               his stammer.
OBLOMOV: He has a stammer?
TARANTYEV: Yes, he managed a big estate for three years
               but the owner dismissed him in the end –
               because of his stammer. Which is why he's
               back in St Petersburg working in an office.
OBLOMOV: Are you sure I could rely on him? I mean,
               I've nothing against men with stammers but
               this is a big –
TARANTYEV: Trust me, he's the soul of honour. He'd do
               anything to serve his employer.
OBLOMOV: How come - if he's working in an office -
               that he can find time to go to Oblomovka?
TARANTYEV: He'd take leave of course. I could bring
               him here to meet you. Mind you, he
               wouldn't do it for nothing.
OBLOMOV: I wouldn't expect that.
TARANTYEV: May you could give him his travelling
               expenses and so much per day. And then
               when the business is over, you pay him an
               agreed sum.
OBLOMOV: (RELIEVED) You know, I really am
               obliged to you. You're saving me a great
               deal of trouble. What did you say his name
               was?

TARANTYEV: (IMPRESSIVELY) Isay Fomitch Zatyorty.
            (PAUSE) I'll talk to him to-morrow and
            then bring him round to see you for dinner.
            How's that?
OBLOMOV: Perfect!
TARANTYEV: He's a great gourmet so make sure you lay
            on something special – and don't stint on
            the champagne.
OBLOMOV: I won't.

            (TARANTYEV LEAVES.)
            (OBLOMOV GIVES A SIGH OF RELIEF.)

OBLOMOV: Thank heavens that's sorted. What a load
            off my mind!

            (PAUSE)

OBLOMOV: But what about Olga? I'll have to tell her. I
            can't lie. She deserves better. I love her. She
            loves me.

            (HEROIC PAUSE. HE RISES FROM THE
            BED)

OBLOMOV: There's nothing for it. I shall have to go and
            see her.

            (BLACKOUT.)
            (THE RUSSIAN FOLK SONG OLGA
            SANG IN ACT ONE)
            (LIGHTS UP ON OLGA STANDING IN
            SILENCE)
            (THE MUSIC FADES)
            (OBLOMOV ENTERS)

OBLOMOV: Olga!
OLGA: Ilya!

            (THEY KISS)

OLGA: I was beginning to think you might not
            come.

OBLOMOV:	Is your aunt here?
OLGA:	Not just now.
OBLOMOV:	That's just as well.
OLGA:	But we're expecting her back soon.
OBLOMOV:	Oh dear. The fact is - I've had a letter – about the estate. But it's not good news.
OLGA:	What do you mean?
OBLOMOV:	There's a lot less money than I expected. But there's no need to worry. It's all in hand. I consulted Tarantyev this morning and he's recommended a certain Isay Fomitch Zatyorty for the job. He's going to go down and sort it out.
OLGA:	You mean a perfect stranger is going to collect the peasants' taxes, settle their disputes and look after the sale of corn?
OBLOMOV:	Tarantyev assures me he's the soul of honour. His only problem is that he has a stammer. Well, you can't hold that against him, can you?
OLGA:	(COLDLY) No, you can't.
OBLOMOV:	(QUICKLY) I mean, if I don't send him, I'll have to go myself. And even if I did go, I'd be useless. Much better to leave it in the hands of an expert. Besides, I'd hate being in the country without you. But just as soon as things are settled and my agent gets the house rebuilt and the income sorted out then I shall be free to talk to your aunt and then we can be together, never to part again. After all, it's only a year.
OLGA:	(BREAKING DOWN) No! No! I can't bear it any more.

(SHE BURSTS INTO TEARS)

OBLOMOV:	Olga – please – don't cry.
OLGA:	It's hopeless, hopeless!
OBLOMOV:	Maybe you're right. Maybe I shouldn't trust this Isay Fomitch Zatyorty. Maybe I should go down myself. Or maybe I should go with him and –
OLGA:	You will never go down there.

OLGA: I am duly punished for my pride. I've relied too much on my power to change you. It's not your fault but I couldn't. I thought I could revive you and make you live for my sake. But you died long ago.

OBLOMOV: Olga, I love you!

OLGA: I love you too, which only makes it worse. But tell me, Ilya – do you really believe that in a year's time you will have put your affairs and your life in order?

(PAUSE)

OBLOMOV: But, Olga, my darling Olga –

OLGA: I don't want a protestation of love, I just want an answer. Am I right or not?

OBLOMOV: (QUIETLY) No, you are right.

OLGA: Even if we did marry, what would come of it? You would still sink into deeper and deeper sleep every day. I love life and I hate the idea of growing old. With you I'd be going to bed in the evening, thanking God that the day had passed so quickly, and then wake up in the morning wishing that the coming day would be like the one before. I would pine away, I would die. And what for?

OBLOMOV: (TRYING TO BE BRAVE) Well, then, it's goodbye.

(OLGA STARTS TO CRY AGAIN)

OBLOMOV: Olga –

OLGA: No, don't worry about me. I will cry it all out now and then I won't cry any more. So please – don't try to stop my tears. Just go away – please! Whatever it is that I need I have to recognise that you cannot give it to me.

OBLOMOV: I'm so sorry.

| OLGA: | Who laid this curse on you, Ilya? You are kind, intelligent, affectionate and – you are doomed. And there is no name for the evil that has ruined you. |
| OBLOMOV: | (SOFTLY) Oh, yes, there is. (PAUSE) Oblomovism. And now – goodbye – |

(HE STARTS TO LEAVE BUT SUDDENLY GIVES A GASP AND COLLAPSES TO THE FLOOR.)
(OLGA RUNS TO HIM)

| OLGA: | Ilya! Ilya! (CALLING) Come quickly, Mr Oblomov has fainted. |

(BLACKOUT)
(A BABBLE OF CONFUSED VOICES AND SOUNDS.
(AMONG THE PROMINENT REPEATED PHRASES ARE TARANTYEV SAYING: "Isay Fomitch Zatyorty." ZAHAR SAYING "Anything rather than visit the bloody place" AND OLGA SAYING: "You died long ago, Ilya".
(EVENTUALLY THE BABBLE RECEDES)
(OBLOMOV LYING ASLEEP IN BED IN HIS DARKENED ROOM WEARING HIS OLD DRESSING GOWN)
(HE SIGHS CONTENTEDLY)

| OBLOMOV: | Ah, yes, how I still love you, my home, my lovely childhood home, my Oblomovka. |

(A WOMAN IN THE DARKNESS CALLS: Ilya! Ilya!)

| OBLOMOV: | And look - here comes nursey! She wants me to put my stockings on but I won't let her! I kick my legs and say I don't want to get up. I'm never going to get up! |

(LIGHTS CHANGE. THE WOMAN BY
HIS SIDE IS AGAFYA)

AGAFYA:	Mr Oblomov – Mr Oblomov!
OBLOMOV:	(SUDDENLY AWAKE) Where – what is it?
AGAFYA:	I've brought you some soup.
OBLOMOV:	Oh, thank you, thank you so much.
AGAFYA:	The doctor says you've been making good progress.
OBLOMOV:	Yes – yes – I suppose I have.

(HE STARTS TO EAT THE SOUP)

AGAFYA:	And my brother says that Isay Fomitch Zatyorty is working wonders on your estate.
OBLOMOV:	He's certainly been sending me money which is the main thing. Otherwise I wouldn't be able to pay you the rent – or for my food. The trouble is – I have no sense of time any more.
AGAFYA:	It's six months and three days since you were brought back here.
OBLOMOV:	Six months! The time's passed in such a blur.
AGAFYA:	That's because you've been in a fever. I'll be making you some nice supper soon, Mr Oblomov. Pickled cabbage and salmon.
OBLOMOV:	That's splendid!
AGAFYA:	There's no sturgeon to be had though. I've been to all the shops but there isn't any.
OBLOMOV:	You never stop working, do you?
AGAFYA:	So you always say.
OBLOMOV:	I love to watch you. Whether you're pounding cinnamon or washing the floor or baking a pie – you're always so full of life.
AGAFYA:	Full of work more like.
OBLOMOV:	You have been so good to me. I wouldn't have survived without you.

(HE FINISHES THE SOUP)

AGAFYA:	So how was the soup?

75

OBLOMOV:	Delicious – as always. Agafya Matveyevna –
AGAFYA:	(TAKING BOWL) What is it?
OBLOMOV:	I was just wondering – tell me – what would you say if I said I loved you?
AGAFYA:	Why not? God commanded us to love everyone.
OBLOMOV:	And what if I kissed you?
AGAFYA:	But it isn't Easter week!
OBLOMOV:	All the same –
AGAFYA:	All the same – I should go. There's the supper to attend to.

(SHE LEAVES)

| OBLOMOV: | I do hope I haven't embarrassed her. But there's something so warm and so comforting about being here in her cosy house and eating her nourishing food. When I think back to my other life, well, it seems like a dream. All that gossip, all those parties and – dear, demanding Olga Sergeyevna. And now – |

(HE YAWNS)

| OBLOMOV: | Mmm… I do believe I can smell the fish. |

(ZAHAR ENTERS AT SPEED.)

ZAHAR:	It's Mr Stolz!
OBLOMOV:	Mr Stolz!
ZAHAR:	(DRYLY) Yes, your oldest and dearest friend, remember.
OBLOMOV:	But he's abroad.
ZAHAR:	Well, even he can't stay abroad forever. He's asking to see you. God knows why but he is.
OBLOMOV:	Show him in.
ZAHAR:	No need.
STOLZ:	(ENTERING) Ilya!
OBLOMOV:	Andrey! Dearest Andrey! This calls for a celebration. Zahar, bring us some wine!

OBLOMOV: I'd no idea you were back.

STOLZ: I only got back yesterday. I'm sorry to hear
             you'd been so ill.

OBLOMOV: (SHRUGS) These things happen. So how
             was Paris?

STOLZ: Fascinating. Pity you never managed to get
             there.

OBLOMOV: Well, yes…

(THE GLASSES ARE FULL AND HE
RAISES HIS GLASS)

OBLOMOV: Your good health!

STOLZ: And yours.

(ZAHAR LEAVES THEM ALONE.)
(SLIGHTLY AWKWARD PAUSE)

OBLOMOV: Well, you did say "now or never", didn't
             you? So I suppose it looks like being
             "never". But I'm not the same as I was,
             Andrey. My business affairs, thank Heaven,
             are in order. My plans for the estate are
             nearly finished. Of course I got behind
             schedule because –

STOLZ: Because of the business with Olga?

OBLOMOV: You know?

STOLZ: Of course. We met up in Paris where she
             and her aunt went soon after…

OBLOMOV: Soon after she'd learned her mistake, you
             mean? So you know everything?

STOLZ: Everything. (PAUSE) I'm so sorry.

OBLOMOV: (SLOWLY) How is she?

STOLZ: She's recovered. It's been a long and painful
             process. But we talked a great deal and –
             and now she's happy.

OBLOMOV: I'm so pleased.

STOLZ: But I have to say that we are both concerned
             for you.

OBLOMOV: For me?

STOLZ:	We worry about your future.
OBLOMOV:	Oh, I'm fine. Please don't bother yourselves.
STOLZ:	Ilya, you've not been well. It's a warning. You know that if you don't change your way of life, you're heading for a stroke. You have to stir yourself.
OBLOMOV:	And do what?
STOLZ:	Go down to your estate. It's summer now which is the best time to visit and –
OBLOMOV:	But I've an agent. He's already sent me fifteen hundred roubles this year.
STOLZ:	Ilya, you're being robbed. Fifteen hundred roubles from an estate that's twenty thousand!
OBLOMOV:	Well, to be fair, it was more than fifteen hundred. But the agent took a fee for his labours out of the money received for the sale of corn.
STOLZ:	How much?
OBLOMOV:	I don't remember.
STOLZ:	So who recommended this agent to you?
OBLOMOV:	Tarantyev!
STOLZ:	Tarantyev! That crook!
OBLOMOV:	But you weren't around to give me advice so I didn't have anyone to turn to. And, after all, he's the landlady's brother.
STOLZ:	The landlady's brother!
OBLOMOV:	Please don't keep repeating everything I say. She's a very nice woman with two children and she works very hard –
STOLZ:	Let's get this clear. Tarantyev has got you on a long-term contract into this dump of a flat doubtless on some exorbitant rent –
OBLOMOV:	I like it here!
STOLZ:	And on top of that he's got some crooked crony of his to go down and rip off your estate.
OBLOMOV:	(MEEKLY) I think that's rather a crude way of looking at it.
STOLZ:	I need to have words with Mr Tarantyev…
OBLOMOV:	Very well but please – don't upset Agafya Matveyevna.

STOLZ:	Just how close to this woman are you, Ilya?
OBLOMOV:	What do you mean?
STOLZ:	You – you haven't made her any promises?
OBLOMOV:	No, no, I've told her how fond of her I am of course, but -
STOLZ:	So maybe I should talk to her as well.
OBLOMOV:	There's no need.
STOLZ:	Ilya, you're blushing.
OBLOMOV:	Don't be absurd!
STOLZ:	I'm going to seek out Tarantyev right away and get to the bottom of all this.
OBLOMOV:	But please – be careful…

(LIGHTS CHANGE.)
(OBLOMOV ALONE DOZING IN BED.)
(TARANTYEV BURSTS IN)

TARANTYEV:	I want a word with you!
OBLOMOV:	What about?
TARANTYEV:	That stuck-up German sod's been poking his nose into things that don't concern him.
OBLOMOV:	You're talking about my best friend!
TARANTYEV:	Spare me that crap. Just don't blame me if Isay Fomitch Zatyorty gets the hump and leaves you and your estate in the lurch. But that's not the half of it. That German bastard's suggested you're being ripped off for staying in this flat.
OBLOMOV:	But I'm very happy here.
TARANTYEV:	Exactly. Which is why I can't imagine why he's questioning the IOU.
OBLOMOV:	(BLANKLY) What IOU?
TARANTYEV:	(PRODUCING A PIECE OF PAPER) The one you gave my sister for ten thousand roubles – for all she's done for you.
OBLOMOV:	But I don't recall ever having –
TARANTYEV:	That's your signature. You'll be telling me next you were drunk at the time
OBLOMOV:	Or still in a fever. I – it's the only explanation.
TARANTYEV:	Doesn't matter. My sister does what I tell her so if you cut up rough then I'll cut up rougher and –

79

(STOLZ NOW APPEARS WITH A
TEARFUL AGAFYA

STOLZ:	Ilya, Agafya Matveyevna wants to say something.
AGAFYA:	I'm sorry about all this, Mr Oblomov. You don't owe me anything.
TARANTYEV:	Hold your tongue, sister.
AGAFYA:	No, I'm very fond of Mr Oblomov and when Mr Stolz told me about this IOU, I couldn't believe it.
TARANTYEV:	Sister, don't you dare –
AGAFYA:	But it's not true –
TARANTYEV:	(THREATENING) I said – hold your peace, you stupid bitch!

(HE GOES FOR HER. THEY STRUGGLE.
STOLZ TRIES TO INTERVENE.)
(OBLOMOV IS HORRIFIED)
(HE RISES FROM HIS BED AND PULLS
TARANTYEV OFF HIS SISTER.)

OBLOMOV:	Leave her alone!
TARANTYEV:	Says who?
OBLOMOV:	I do. Leave her alone!
TARANTYEV:	Oh, give me a break, you useless pathetic –

(OBLOMOV HITS HIM – HARD)
(TARANTYEV FALLS TO THE
GROUND GROANING.)
(THE OTHERS STARE.)

OBLOMOV:	Oh, my God, I've hit him. I've hit him.

(BLACKOUT)
(LIGHTS UP ON STOLZ SITTING BY
OBLOMOV, WHO IS BACK IN HIS
BED.)

STOLZ:	I shall miss you, Ilya.
OBLOMOV:	No, no, I know my limitations, I'm much happier here. Being looked after by Agafya

	Matveyevna. I can't thank you enough for getting her brother off my back.
STOLZ:	You're the one who punched him. He won't bother you again.
OBLOMOV:	But you also found the time to sort out my estate and get rid of Isay Fomitch Zatyorty.
STOLZ:	The new agent's an honest man. It really needs for you to be there but – well, it's not going to happen, is it?
OBLOMOV:	(SIGHS) No. But thank you anyway.
STOLZ:	I felt I owed you that.
OBLOMOV:	Why?
STOLZ:	There's something I haven't told you.
OBLOMOV:	I think I can guess.
STOLZ:	Olga and I are engaged to be married.
OBLOMOV:	That's much the best thing.
STOLZ:	She – she's changed. She's grown up and – well, we fell in love in Paris. And when I realised your engagement to her was definitely over, I – I asked her to marry me.
OBLOMOV:	I think you were always made for each other.
STOLZ:	We intend to travel.
OBLOMOV:	Very wise.
STOLZ:	I wish I could change you, Ilya.
OBLOMOV:	No, really, I'm not worth the trouble.

(HE SMILES. THE LIGHTS DARKEN AGAIN)
(STOLZ HAS GONE)
(OBLOMOV SETTLES BACK IN HIS BED PULLING HIS DRESSING GOWN ABOUT HIM)
(RETURN OF THE COUNTRY MUSIC FROM START)
(ZAHAR AND AGAFYA APPEAR IN THE HALF LIGHT BEHIND OBLOMOV'S BED)
(HE SMILES HAPPILY AS THEY SPEAK:)

ZAHAR:	She's made you a delicious macaroni with Parmesan cheese..

OBLOMOV:	Ah...
AGAFYA:	Here's your fresh coffee, my love.
OBLOMOV:	Ah...
ZAHAR:	Here's the cigar she promised you...
OBLOMOV:	Ah...
AGAFYA:	Tomorrow I'll be making fish soup – and chicken pie.
OBLOMOV:	Ah...

(HE YAWNS CONTENTEDLY. THE MUSIC CONTINUES)

OBLOMOV: I think this was how it was always meant to end. I lie cosily here in my bed attended by my faithful servant and my lovely wife and my lovely little son. We've called him Andrey in honour of the only true friend I ever had. He and Olga still write to me about all the places they've been. Andrey once said it started with my inability to put on my socks and it's ended with my inability to live. But I really don't care. I feel like a mole sleeping in its burrow – and I don't ever ever want to be dragged back into the world outside. This is like being back as a child in Oblomovka with nursey and mummy – only this time I don't have to get up – ever.

(THE MUSIC AND THE LIGHT START TO FADE AWAY)

OBLOMOV: I'm going to stay here forever and ever until one day quietly simply without fuss, I'll go off into one last final good long sleep.

(SILENCE AND DARKNESS)

THE END